Hero

Catherine R. Johnson

To S. W. and E. M. Johnson

OXFORD
UNIVERSITY PRESS

Great Clarendon Street, Oxford OX2 6DP

Oxford University Press is a department of the University of Oxford.
It furthers the University's objective of excellence in research, scholarship,
and education by publishing worldwide in

Oxford New York

Auckland Bangkok Buenos Aires
Cape Town Chennai Dar es Salaam Delhi Hong Kong Istanbul
Karachi Kolkata Kuala Lumpur Madrid Melbourne Mexico City Mumbai
Nairobi São Paulo Shanghai Singapore Taipei Tokyo Toronto

With an associated company in Berlin

Oxford is a registered trade mark of Oxford University Press
in the UK and in certain other countries

First published 2001
First published in this edition 2002

British Library Cataloguing in Publication Data available

ISBN 0 19 275197 2

1 3 5 7 9 10 8 6 4 2

Typeset by AFS Image Setters Ltd, Glasgow

Printed in Great Britain

ONE

Hero had never hit anyone that hard before. She felt her knuckles stinging and watched as Daniel swayed across the courtyard and finally fell clumsily against the wall of The Feathers. Hero felt suddenly scared. What if she had really hurt him? Knocked out his teeth. Shattered his jaw.

She had hoped she'd feel triumphant. Feel how Pa looked in the engraving hung over the fireplace in the saloon. The one that said 'Gentleman John of Barbados felling Dutch Sam at Blackheath'. In that particular picture, the artist had managed to make the man half naked with his fists up actually look like Pa. Not just a shaded-in white man or a thick-lipped cartoon.

Daniel rubbed his cheek and stood up shakily. His little brother Sam and his big sister Rachel helped him.

'You get her, Danny.' Rachel dabbed at him with her dirty handkerchief.

'But, Rachel! I knocked him down, that counts as a win!' Hero shouted.

'He was bein' easy on you, weren't you, Dan. Dan?' Rachel slapped him lightly around the face. 'He thought you were a girl an' not a gorilla.'

'Listen, you.' Hero was a foot taller than Rachel. 'My fight's with you, not your kid brother. It weren't him who pushed me over in front of everyone. It's not him who's got a mouth like the Fleet sewer.'

Rachel smiled sweetly. 'Well, now your grandpa's dead it won't be long before you're back on the street where you belong.'

Hero blew on her knuckles and stepped back ready to hit her if she had to. She kept moving, stepping backwards and forwards in a little shuffling dance that made the shiny black taffetta of the mourning dress rustle on the stone flags. She wished Rachel would rush at her, but Rachel had other ways of fighting.

Daniel rubbed the side of his face. It was red and Hero thought she had broken the skin.

'Leave it, Rachel,' Daniel said. 'She won an' you know it. Fair an' square. She knocked me down an' that's the rules.' He put his hand out to shake hers. 'Fair an' square.'

Hero smiled. 'Sorry, Dan. About your face.'

Rachel shook the skirt of her black satin frock and pulled her bonnet straight on her head. Her face was as red as her hair and when she scowled she looked just like a miniature of her mother. She led Sam away and spat hard before she turned out of the courtyard and onto Old Compton Street.

'Sorry about Rachel.' Daniel brushed the dust off his black jacket. Hero shook her head and passed Daniel his cap. 'You watch my ma an' all,' Daniel said while they stood close. 'Some of this family never liked your pa. You know that well enough.'

'Thanks, Daniel.' Hero put her hand out to shake his. 'You're a good friend.'

Hero followed him out into the street where the shops were lit up and walked round to the front of The Feathers. Above the door a sign in best gilt paint said 'Prop. Reuben da Costa and Son'. The noise from the funeral party spilled out of the pub and carried down the street. Hero reckoned all the swell mob of London were packed into The Feathers tonight. All for her grandpa. Hero counted four waiting curricles and two cabs. She smiled and Lord Camelford's coachman winked at her. She scowled and folded her arms tight across her chest.

Hero stopped in the doorway and looked south down the Charing Cross Road. The city was cooling and the worst of the high stink that rose from the street and out of every house in summer was receding, fading into the darkness. She looked towards the Seven Dials half expecting Grandpa Reuben would shuffle out of Earlham Street towards The Feathers. Hero looked for him through the crowds of people and street sellers. Children turning cartwheels in the dust and crossing sweepers lifting the horse and dog turds and carefully bagging them up for sale later.

But Hero had seen the coffin with Grandpa Reuben inside it lowered into the earth next to her mother in the little Jews' Cemetery off the Mile End Road. She had seen her father and five others of the best prizefighters in town carry his coffin in through the gates and lay it down. He wouldn't be coming home tonight.

Hero sighed. The shops were lit up, the street singers were singing, the beggars were begging. It could be any Wednesday that had ever happened. She turned to go back inside. Pa would need help clearing this lot up. The swell mob and the followers of the fancy might be high rollers with fine clothes and town houses in the West End, but, as Pa said, they like to come to us and make a mess. To sing too loud, to drink too much, and to puke on our floors.

Hero froze. A man was stepping towards her from Shaftesbury Avenue. It was the crossing sweeper who usually sat at the entrance to Phoenix Court and called her 'sister'. Pa used to let him have a jug of ale for nothing on Sundays. He was grinning at her and waving. His wide grin showed no teeth and his coat was shredded rags. One arm was completely bare shiny skin and above his arm on his naked shoulder Hero could see a lumpy raised scar. From the safety of The Feather's door it appeared as a smudge, a growth. But Hero had seen it close up and knew what it was. A brand. Like Pa's. Hero turned away, so afraid her skin prickled, and ran straight inside the pub, pushing through the crowds of young gentlemen and into the saloon where she ran smack into the black satin upholstered bosom of Rachel's mother.

'Hero da Costa!' Mrs Silver pushed her away. 'Clumsiest girl in all London, I should say! Are you shaking, girl? You should be! What have you done to my Daniel?' Hero was taller than Mrs Silver too and she glared at her. 'On this day of all days! Why, my Uncle Reuben must have been punch drunk to think that anything could come of you people!'

Hero wanted to sock her. If Grandpa had been alive he would have sent her out of the pub. Sent her back to her poky house on the other side of London.

'Desiree! I'm sure it was nothing. You know what the children are like.' Pa had come out from behind the bar and took Mrs Silver's arm. She shook him off.

'You can't sweet talk me. Not like you did my poor cousin Lily. Look at this girl, this giant of yours. No wonder my Lily died giving birth to that! Come, Dan, Rachel!' She turned and was gone.

Hero didn't cry. She wanted to, but crying was for ragheads like Rachel. She felt the tears welling up behind her eyes and she squeezed her hands into fists.

'Keep all your hate in there, Hero,' Reuben would say, holding her hands, and she could feel the hate she had for that woman buzzing inside her fists. Hero ran upstairs tripping halfway up on the black mourning dress and tearing the shiny material around the hem. She shut the door of her room and punched into her lumpy mattress. Again and again and again, making clouds of dust fly up and hang in the air.

'I didn't kill you, Ma! I never!' She punched and punched until her hands were numb and the hate had all come out. Her eyes were only slightly damp.

The one picture of Ma was in Pa's room, rolled up tight with some papers inside the writing desk by his bed. It had been on the wall but the sunlight had begun to fade it, so it had been put away. Hero thumped across the landing and pushed open the door. She scrabbled around in the top left hand drawer and pulled out the bundle of papers and unrolled her mother's portrait.

Lily Juliet stared out of the smudgy portrait with large, soft brown eyes and pale, pale skin. Ma was frail, Grandpa Reuben said. She looked well enough in the picture, Hero thought. Pa always said Ma had wanted a baby so much he thought she'd burst. It wasn't true what Aunt Silver said and Hero knew it.

When she was younger Hero would come up here and talk to Lily Juliet. Hero sat down on Pa's bed and looked and looked at the picture and Ma said, of course you never killed me, Hero. Hero smiled and stroked her face. Then she kissed Ma on the cheek and went to change.

She took off the mourning and squeezed herself into her usual blue cotton dress. It had been new at Easter but it already cut deep into her armpits. At Whitsun, only a week past, Hero had gone with her friend Sara to the apothecary in Lisle Street to ask for something to stop her growing. Sara said she thought they must have something, but Hero soon realized the only reason Sara was so keen on that particular apothecary was the apprentice. Sara was smitten with boys regularly. 'Isn't he just a darling, Hero?' Hero hadn't yet met any boy—especially a usually spotty-faced apprentice—that she would describe as a darling. 'I could knock him out with my little finger, Sar!'

Hero eased the seam of her dress apart gently with her fingers and thought that if she didn't have to raise her arms she'd be just fine. Downstairs the swells were leaving and Hero set to work with Ez, the pot boy, and Mary who came in twice a week, scrubbing lordly vomit from under a table.

It was another hour before they were finished. Pa sent Mary home and Ez went to his bed in the back room. Pa lit a candle and sat down. He looked as if he'd been awake all week.

'Hero,' he said, 'come and sit with me.'

'I'm tired, Pa.' She yawned as if proof were needed.

'A few minutes, that's all.'

Hero sat down.

'There's things I must tell you. Now Grandpa's dead . . . things might be . . . different.'

'Can't it wait, Pa? Till tomorrow?' Hero didn't want the family history. She didn't want to know how or why or where Pa had come from or what had happened to him. She didn't want to think about slavery or being kidnapped. Or being sold. Being sold. She shivered. For Hero, history started when Grandpa Reuben met Pa in 1795. Pa became Gentleman John of Barbados, and married Reuben's daughter Lily Juliet. And if Ma had lived it would all have been happy ever after.

'Hero.' Pa sighed. 'Things are going to change.' Save me from change, Hero said to herself. He smiled at her.

'Pa, can we not talk in the morning? Grandpa's just buried and my hands are raw with scrubbing. We've got all the tomorrows now, Pa.'

'That's what I'm worried about, Hero. That's just what I'm worried about. You may be the biggest, the bravest girl I know in London, but that won't stop some people,' Pa shook his head, ' . . . some people.'

Hero went upstairs quickly before he could go on, but even though she was tired she didn't sleep straight away. She listened for Pa coming up the stairs but she never heard him. She didn't hear anything until some time early the next morning, and that was the sound of a detachment of officers, quick-marched from Bow Street, breaking down the solid mahogany door of The Feathers and reading out a warrant for Pa's arrest.

Hero ran down the stairs in her nightclothes. Ez was up already, hiding behind the bar counter. A tall brown-haired man stood facing Pa, two others held his arms tight behind his back. The tall man stood inches from Pa's face, shouting at him. Pa didn't move. The shouting man was shouting about property rights, about absconding, about loss of chattels. Then the officers pulled John da Costa, 'Lately of The Feathers public house, and rightful property of Mr Owen, Fairwinds, Barbados', out of The Feathers and down towards the Strand.

'Hero, I'll be back, I'll be back soon!' Pa shouted after her and Hero ran after him, nightshirt flapping.

'Pa? Pa!' It was too late, the officers closed tight around him and marched him away.

Hero stood next to Ez in the gaping hole that was their front door and watched as the knot of men disappeared down St Martin's Lane. 'He's done nothing! Nothing!'

TWO

'Shake yourself, girl!' Mrs Desiree Silver pinched Hero's cheek hard. Hero felt her skin smart but she couldn't move. The cart had stopped and Mrs Silver hauled herself down to the pavement. She shouted something into the house and soon the three huge young men on the back of the cart were unloading all the contents of The Feathers into the Silvers' house in White Kennet Street.

There was Pa's bed and writing desk and wash jug from his bedroom. There was Grandpa Reuben's two best chairs and all his books. There was the chest of clothes that had belonged to Lily Juliet, her wedding dress of yellowed satin and the slippers too. The belts that Pa and Grandpa won in fights, the cash box for locking up takings at the end of every day. The pictures off the walls, everything. Hero sat numb on the cart and watched Pa's writing table sticking in the door frame of the Silvers' dark, narrow, house.

'Hero! You've hands, girl!' Mrs Silver clapped hers. 'Get down at once and show willing! Your soft-headed father's not here to carry you now. I'm afraid we all work harder than you lot up west.'

Hero slid down off the cart and looked up at the house. The windows were black with dirt and the house looked worn out. Five storeys stretched up in front of her. The back parlour was Uncle Silver's workroom where old clothes were sorted into good, bad, and rags. He used to have a warehouse and shop off Rag Fair but times were hard—as Aunt Silver was forever telling anyone who would listen—and the warehouse had been sold last summer.

Hero had been trying to convince herself that none of this was happening. That Pa would turn up riding a shiny bay horse and take her home. 'It was a silly mistake, my darling.' He'd be grinning at her and then she'd jump up behind him and they'd go home. Mrs Silver would be left completely, utterly, dumbstruck and Pa would make her send everything back.

Mrs Silver had come with the cart before Hero had dressed. Hero and Ez were still frozen with shock and had only just begun sweeping the splinters and shards of wood that had been the front door into a neat little pile. Ez had said how his dad, if he was remembering rightly, had been gone for two weeks when his ma just thought he'd gone over to Holloway looking for work. He came back, Ez said, with no shirt and his ma had clocked him and had a good laugh, Ez said. Hero didn't smile. Maybe this was one of the changes Pa had been talking about. Maybe Pa was involved in thieving or maybe he owed a load of money. Hero felt worse.

Hero had just convinced herself that there was no way her pa would thieve, when there, in the broken door, stood Aunt Silver. She was round and red headed, still head to toe in black mourning with an old-fashioned tie bonnet on her head and hard black boots on her feet. Three large men, tall and wide, one with sea boots, the others barefoot, climbed down from the cart and walked straight in, taking everything that wasn't nailed down and piling it into the cart.

'Hey, hey, that's Mr da Costa's stuff.' Ez drew himself up and stood in their way but no one took any notice of him. They swatted him sideways and after being knocked to the floor a couple of times Ez kept his mouth shut. Hero helped him up and hugged him hard. She said nothing and concentrated on not crying in front of Aunt Silver, who looked around the saloon smiling in her shiny black-beetle boots.

'You can't take our stuff, Aunt Silver. Pa'll be coming home soon, I'm sure of it.' Hero leant against the bar like

Pa did and tried to sound reasonable and responsible. She cleared her throat and held her nightgown closed at the top.

'I know we're young, but me and Ez are all right, ain't we, Ez.' Ez nodded.

'Hero, your pa won't be needing any of this, and as I'm all your family now—'

'Pa's not dead! He's not! It's just the officers that took him away!'

Hero felt the ground softening under her feet, the bar she was leaning on was suddenly swallowing her. Pa wasn't dead. Pa couldn't be dead. 'I'll go now and fetch him, Aunt.' Hero shuffled into the street in her night shirt. 'I'll go and fetch him now.' She stepped out into Cambridge Circus, where the world had started Thursday morning as usual. The fruit boy yelled at her and the girl with the pail of milk laughed. It wasn't until she cut her soft, normally shod, feet on a sharp stone that she realized she wasn't dressed and that everyone was staring.

'Hero! Hero!' Her aunt shouted at her. 'Who said anything about dead.' Mrs Silver rolled her eyes. 'You're so hot headed, girl! Your pa's gone back to where he came from and you should be grateful you're not with him. Now set to it and pack. You're living with us now and lucky to be so!'

And Hero da Costa, the bravest, biggest girl in London, had crumpled up into a ball by the side of the road and wept.

The front door and the hall of the Silvers' house was blocked with men and furniture, so Hero swung the blanket which had her clothes tied up in it off the cart, pulled her wrap around herself, and shuffled down the area stairs to the kitchen.

The kitchen was dark, like a cave, with the occasional glint of metal and firelight. There was a heavy greasy smell of yesterday's cooking and the floor stuck to the bottom of Hero's shoes. In the middle of the gloom the Silvers' cook was making bread. Hero squeezed round her and up the back stairs into the house. Up she went, past the workshop, to the first floor. The smell of unwashed cloth and other people's dirt hung in the air. Hero could hear the voices of the girls at work and thought that however hard an innkeeper's work was, it rated better than skimming through old woollen breeches stiff with dirt and stinking heavy petticoats.

Hero had been at the Silvers' often for Passover and New Year, and she pushed open the door to the upstairs drawing room and sat down, pulling her bundle of clothes onto her lap. She sat there for some time, listening to the noise of the men outside and the bumps and knocks as they unloaded the cart. There was breaking—a beautiful heavenly tinkling—from the sound Hero reckoned it to be the best gilt mirror from the saloon in The Feathers. Mrs Silver swore at the men and screamed how she would dock their fee. That the mirror was next to priceless and had been in her family for years, she said. Hero remembered the day Pa bought it, off the silverer in St Martin's Lane.

Hero looked down at the Silvers' green and red Ankara carpet. It was worn right through near the door, but the pattern was nice, vines and birds and curls, it was restful and soothing and she could almost forget this morning had happened. Hero followed the pattern with her eyes then stopped. Rachel had been sitting in the far window seat all this time. Hero almost jumped.

'Rachel! I didn't see you there.'

Rachel snapped shut the book she was reading and grinned.

'Hero, I've just been reading about you, in this.' Rachel held up the book. It was a black-bound Bible.

'I said to Ma we should put you on the next ship bound for the West Indies with your father, but my ma's so soft hearted she thought you'd be better off with us.' Rachel looked up and smiled. 'Don't think it's going to be easy though, not for one minute. I've just been reading what it says about you lot in here.' She waved the book. 'You're cursed. The curse of Ham. Look for yourself. It's your own fault an' that. You're cursed and we're chosen. "The servant of servants"—it's your destiny. It says so. God says so.'

Hero didn't move. She stared at the worn patch in the Silvers' Ankara carpet and felt her eyes prickling with tears. Was Pa really on a slaver for the other side of the world? She must be cursed. Yesterday she would've pulled herself up and hit Rachel hard. I'll show you cursed, she would have said and knocked Rachel Silver onto the carpet and into oblivion. Today she shivered a little sigh like Sara's lap dog, Buff.

Rachel came close and stuck her freckled face inches from Hero's. 'I'm not scared of you, Hero da Costa!' Rachel dropped the Bible in Hero's lap and flounced out. Hero had missed out on religion. With Grandpa Jewish and Pa never baptized she'd only been to church with Sara. Grandpa took her up to synagogue sometimes but she'd never been that good at reading. She could read the suppliers' dockets at the pub and Pa had showed her letters, but she'd never sat down with the Bible. The pages were thin as muslin and edged with gold and the writing was the smallest she had ever seen. She didn't need to read the Curse of Ham. She knew what it meant. Ham was one of Noah's sons. She knew the story of the flood at least. Three sons Noah had, Ham, Shem, and Japeth. Only them and their wives to make up for all the people drowned in the great flood. Anyway, after the flood, Ham had looked at his father naked, and for that God cursed him. And Ham, as everyone knew, was the ancestor of every dark-skinned man alive.

Hero sat and listened to the men unloading the cart. It was only a matter of time before Mrs Silver found her sitting and gave her something to do so she put the Bible down on the chair, tucked her bundle of clothes under the table, and went to help. Rachel was dancing on the pavement in Lily Juliet's satin slippers. Hero couldn't look. Pa's writing desk had been carried down the front area and Hero hurried after it for the picture of Lily Juliet.

She scrabbled in the drawers but there were sheaves and sheaves of paper curled up tight and ready to spring open all over the area. Hero felt for it, the thicker, textured paper, but Mrs Silver started shouting for her so she squashed the whole lot up together and shoved them under her dress, where no one would notice, and ran back up inside the house.

She was to share her room with Sam, the baby. At supper Aunt Silver announced that thanks to God, Mr Benjamin Silver would be purchasing new premises in Rag Fair and Rachel would have her own room and new gowns for next year when she would be fifteen and have to be thinking seriously about marriage.

THREE

Hero couldn't get to sleep at all. She wriggled in the lumpy bed next to Samuel. He pushed himself sideways and stuck his podgy baby feet into her face.

Hero lay on her back and stared at the ceiling, how it sloped, how the tiny square window poked through, the pattern where the plaster was damp.

She heard the watch at Houndsditch call the hour at midnight, then at one. She heard someone push a hard-wheeled cart over the cobbles towards Bishopsgate and she rolled over and pulled the blanket over her head.

She thought of Pa. How could they take him away, he wasn't a slave. She shuddered. They said someone still owned him. She had heard the name—Owen, it was.

Once she had heard Pa talking to an old American, a beggar—torn coat, hat black with dirt—he'd been in a war he said, fought for the British. Hero heard them talking about slavery and she had stopped listening. She couldn't bear to think of Pa lashed, of Pa bought and sold, of Pa as a thing like a pair of cotton gloves going cheap in Berwick Street market.

She turned onto her back and opened her eyes. The largest damp patch began to spread and darken and Hero realized the whole ceiling was moving. Baby Samuel had vanished, she was in the hold of a vast rolling ship. She could hear the sharp chunk of chains and was aware of twenty, no nearer a hundred, other bodies all pressed in around her. The smell of blood and sweat and shit and piss was solid in the air. There was the creaking of the great ship and the noise of breathing. No wails, no cries, just a hundred breaths, in out, in out, like sighing. She could hear the sea outside, slap-slapping against the dark wooden walls of the ship.

Hero peered into the darkness through the bodies, arms, legs, curves of heads and swore she caught sight of Pa. She tried to wave but the chains that held her arms weren't long enough. He was there, she was sure of it. Out there across the hold somewhere in the tangle of bodies. 'Pa? Pa!'

Her shouts woke Samuel. He cried a long mewling cry, and Hero realized his napkin, clothes, and at least half the bed were soaked. She changed him and soothed him and laid him back down where it was still dry. There was no room in the bed for her now, and anyway it was morning, as good as.

Hero sighed and flipped up the thin curtain over the window. The city was lit pinkish towards the east, glowing, almost alive. Handcarts, donkey carts, wagons, and people passed on the way to Leadenhall or Covent Garden. If she leant right out and spat she could spoil all the milk for the Guildhall. But it was a very long way down. The city was huge, she could make out St Paul's to the west and she could see the river flashing like metal between the gaps in the buildings. Ships' masts stuck up like ragged splinters. Ships . . .

If she pulled herself right up on the window ledge she could see where they clustered all along the river, from the Tower to London Bridge. A thick forest of ships. Hero thought. Of course! That's where Pa would be now. Now! She still had time. She dressed faster than she'd ever dressed before and half fell, half jumped down the narrow stairs towards the front door.

Hero lost her footing in the hall and crashed into the black wooden door heavy with bolts and chains. It rattled hard in its frame and Hero stood up and rubbed her shoulder.

'Girl? Girl!'

Hero looked up and there was Mrs Silver at the top of the stairs. Her nightcap was falling off her head and she was pulling a green shawl around her shoulders.

'What in the heaven's name are you up to?' She started down the stairs towards Hero. 'You had me imagining burglars and cracksmen and all sorts!'

Hero could see Aunt Silver was far from happy.

'I was going out, Aunt.'

'Out? Now?'

'I thought Pa . . . I thought . . . '

Mrs Silver pulled her nightcap into place.

'Do not waste any capacity you may have for thought on your pa!' Mrs Silver glared. 'At this moment, as we— as I—speak, your pa is making his way across the Atlantic Ocean. Your pa, and I do not want to hear his name again, is going back to where he came from, some overheated island in some faraway sea, do you understand!'

'But, Aunt, if he was put on a ship yesterday, it may not have sailed. Sometimes ships don't, sometimes the weather's wrong, sometimes the crew's half cut, I've seen it myself, Aunt . . . '

'Now listen to me, girl! Your pa has gone. Gone! I'm not having you traipsing round the docks telling our business to anyone and everyone.' Mrs Silver rolled her eyes. From the room at the top of the house Samuel had started wailing. 'There! Look what's happened now, with all this carrying on, seeing as you've left poor Sam all alone. Now get up those stairs and sort him out. You've long enough legs, girl, go on.'

Hero was silent. She could hear Samuel yelling his lungs out and she could hear Aunt Silver chivvying her upstairs, but all she could think about was Pa. He couldn't have gone. She had seen him herself yesterday morning, marched off down St Martin's Lane. Only yesterday. If she could just explain . . .

'But, Aunt—'

'No buts, girl, baby's waiting.' Aunt Silver turned towards the stairs.

'Aunt, please. This is important. Pa could still be in

London. I could fetch him, Aunt, everything would go back to normal. Please, Aunt, let me look for Pa.'

It came out of nowhere. The sharp stinging feeling on the side of her face. She thought for an instant that sand or scalding water had been flung at her. Aunt Silver had slapped her.

'I understand, girl, I understand. I understand that you're in my house now and you'll live by my rules. Your pa, your pa is gone. I want you to think of him like your grandpa, or like your mother. He is as good as dead. Remember that. There is plenty of room in the workhouse, and any number of people who'd have shipped you off with your precious pa. They pay more for half breeds like you. So if you want food in your belly and a bed of a night you'd do well to keep your thoughts to yourself and your fat nigger lips shut. All right?'

The words hurt a lot more than her cheek stung. Hero felt as if her insides were folding up. Grandpa dead, Pa dead. She wouldn't go along with that. When Grandpa died she'd seen him, watched as his body grew cold and his skin greyed. She wouldn't pretend her pa was dead too. Mrs Silver was staring into her face. Hero thought. She held her hands by her sides and clenched the right one hard. Never put your thumb inside your fist, Hero, Grandpa said, or you'll bust that along with whoever you're clouting. Mrs Silver had plenty of face to clout. She had a copious double chin that wobbled when she was agitated. It wobbled now. Hero's arm tensed. She stepped back onto her right foot and drew her arm back slowly. Hero thought then that if Aunt Silver had any sense she'd, at the very least, move, back away. But no, Aunt Silver held her ground, one hand holding the shawl together at the neck, the other hand on her hip. Hero let fly.

Punching Mrs Silver wasn't like punching Daniel or the heavy bag of sand that Grandpa had hung up in the basement at The Feathers. Mrs Silver's face crumpled and

Hero felt her knuckles connect with jawbone with a most satisfying crunch. She watched as Aunt Silver keeled over and hit the floor.

Hero stood over her for a second, loosening her fist and wondering if she hadn't killed her, when Aunt Silver began shrieking.

'Oww! Oww! Benjamin! Benjamin!' She called for her husband and struggled to get up, pulling her clothes together. Her face was glowing red all over, not just where she'd been hit and Hero felt a little bit scared.

'As God is my witness, you are no girl! You are never human! Animal! Benjamin, she's an animal!' Uncle Silver was making his way downstairs, Daniel and Rachel were up too, and Hero wished she could just run out of the door and away. But the door was locked. Back door then, she thought, and made a dash down the back stairs to the kitchen faster than the stagecoach with the Dover Mail.

Uncle Silver may have been a small man, but he was a grown man all the same and he caught up with her in the kitchen and held her arms down by her sides. The cook's big son, Mo, came in from the mews and he carried her upstairs to the nursery and they locked the door. 'And don't think you're setting foot outside until you're at least half tame!' Then the household's footsteps receded and it was quiet. They'd even taken Samuel away. 'She might bite his head off!' Rachel said.

Hero was up there all day. She saw Daniel leave for school and she saw a cab come for Rachel and Mrs Silver. She saw Mr Silver walking out with three other black-coated, black-hatted businessmen to view the new rag warehouse he had bought with Pa's money. They didn't waste a minute, Hero thought—they must have been waiting for Grandpa to die all this time. Waiting to get their hands on everything Pa had. She remembered the last time any of them had visited, before Grandpa died. Daniel came on his own. He brought a flask of soup from his mother, he said. Maybe it had been poisoned. Even if that was a little extreme, they had never liked Pa, never even bothered to hide it.

Why hadn't she realized, why hadn't she done anything? They were like crows, the lot of them, sitting cawing, waiting then pecking up the scraps. She hated herself for ever liking any of them. Well, that was only ever Daniel she'd liked, but maybe he was the worst, always hanging around asking questions, always asking about the fighting and what it was like. Pretending to be friendly, all that Cousin Hero this, Cousin Hero that, all the while plotting with his poisonous mother.

Hero fell asleep around lunchtime and dreamt of last New Year's Day at The Feathers. All day she'd been round the markets with Sara fetching apples and mushrooms and nuts. Grandpa had killed four of the chickens they kept in the yard and Mary and Ez plucked them until you couldn't tell snow from chicken feathers. Then Pa made dumplings and they had a feast that night with twenty people all round the table, half of Old Compton Street all sitting down together and so much laughing that Hero woke up crying. And hungry.

She lay in bed listening to her stomach and the shouts of the street sellers: 'Eggs fresh this morning up from Essex, buy six and you'll be rich. Buy twelve, eat them all yourself!' Hero thought of one egg, that would be enough.

She stretched herself and scratched her head. She tried arranging her brown curls back into the piled-up twist she usually wore it in but it felt itchy and greasy. Suddenly she heard a scuffling noise outside the window. It sounded like a pigeon or a starling that was having trouble but then Daniel swung through the open window and landed in a heap on the floor of the room. He was red in the face and sweaty but grinning.

'See, I did it, I made it all the way from school without touching the ground!'

Hero said nothing. He didn't look like a poisoner or a low-life cove.

'Aren't you pleased to see me, then? I could've fallen an' everything.' Daniel brushed the dust off his jacket. Hero thought about hitting him. There were tears almost coming in her eyes. He was just a child; like a puppy, all wide eyes and tricks and stupidness.

'Hero? Hero are you all right?'

'What do you think, Daniel Silver?'

'Sorry, I didn't mean anything.'

'Look at me! Your parents won't let me find Pa. They've shipped him off, they've got rid of him, your sister says! And they've robbed The Feathers, taken everything, and shut me up here! How do you think I am? All right, I suppose. Well, I'm not dead, yet.'

Daniel said nothing. He sat down on the bed and unwrapped a cloth parcel from inside his jacket. Then he laid the contents out carefully. Two round bread rolls, still warm, and one hardboiled egg. 'I thought you'd be hungry.'

Hero reached out slowly and took the egg. She held it in her hand turning it over and over, looking at Daniel. Daniel smiled. He was soft as butter, Hero thought, and she started peeling the brown shell off. 'How do I know they haven't put you up to this.'

'Hero! Come on, can you see my ma happy about me clambering over the rooftops like some sneak's boy?' He pulled his head down into his neck and squeaked like his mother. 'Dan-i-el! Dan-i-el Abraham Silver you get down here at once, before you tear those shilling breeches!'

Hero had to laugh, he was right; Daniel was straight at least.

She bit into the rubbery egg white and it tasted as fine as goose.

'So are you grateful, then?' Daniel asked.

'What for, breakfast in the afternoon?'

'Not just that. Look.' He pointed out of the window.

'Yes?'

'Because, if I can get in here, you can get out, can't you?' Daniel pulled his cap off. 'It's logical.'

'Don't use your schoolbook words on me, Daniel Silver. Whatever logical means, you're not getting me out through there. I've seen it, Dan, it's miles to the street.'

'Look, Hero, I heard all that shouting this morning. You want to see that your father isn't stuck on some boat in the pool of London waiting for the tide or the wind or whatever it is that sailors wait for, don't you?'

Hero tore off some crusty warm roll. She looked at Daniel, and thought he might have a point.

'But why should you care? You could be just like the rest of them. What do you care about Pa?'

Daniel looked hurt, but he was furious. 'Hero da Costa! Your father was the greatest fighter this town has ever seen. Think of all the best fighters—Belasco, Mendoza—and you think of your pa! Gentleman John da Costa! The genuine, the one and only Black Goliath!' Daniel sighed. 'I remember when Grandpa told me about the fight in Hertford with Ben Jasper and the time your pa beat Dutch Sam in forty rounds! Forty rounds and not a mark on him! Gentleman John the Dark Destroyer! Hero, your pa is a national treasure. Just because my parents look at him and see a rich nigger they can sell doesn't mean I don't respect him for what he's done, for who he is.' Daniel leant out of the window. 'I wish I had a father like that. Look at mine! All he wants for me is to sell more rags and more rags, marry a nice girl, sell more rags, and maybe—if I'm lucky—get my name on the board at the synagogue and buy them a nice villa in Tottenham.'

They were quiet. Daniel stood by the open window,

flicking chips of paint out into the street. 'I wanted to run away once,' he said. Hero looked at him. He didn't look the type. 'I used to ask Grandpa Reuben if I could live with you, if he'd train me up. He always said I was too short for the fancy. I reckon he was scared of Mother; she'd sooner die than see me fight. I'm strong though, quick too. There were some tumblers—from Spain they said they were—but I got talking to one of the lads and they lived in Deptford and dyed their hair with walnut to make it black. I could've gone with them.' Daniel looked sad, remembering.

Hero put out her hand for him to shake, she felt rotten for even thinking he wasn't being straight with her. She walked over to the window and looked down. Sheer yellow brick. She looked right and left and saw that Daniel must have inched across from the valley roof. It would be less of a stretch for her because of her height, but she looked down at her dress, her favourite blue cotton, and imagined it tearing on the brick or ripping on the tiles. That was stupid, she reminded herself, who did she think she was—Sara?

'If I can do it, Hero, then you can walk it, you're almost twice my size.'

'Oi, less of that!'

'Come on, you know what I mean.'

'Then let's go, no one will even know I've gone.'

Hero squashed the last of the egg into her mouth and tucked the remaining bread roll into her sleeve.

'Yes, but I think they might miss me at supper. We've got to wait till tonight, it'll be safer—easier in the dark.' He bit his thumb and looked less puppy-like, Hero thought.

'But what if the boat has gone by then?'

Daniel looked serious. 'We've got no choice. We just have to wait.'

FOUR

Hero knew Daniel was right. But the hours before dark moved slower than the Prince of Wales choosing a bride. She watched the river for hours, checking every movement as one ship docked and another departed, praying that Pa was still in London.

Mrs Silver and Rachel returned with coloured boxes of every size and shape, Mr Silver came home, and the lights outside the shops in Houndsditch flared into life. Hero smelled the smells of supper, soup or something hot and warming drifting all the way up five flights of stairs from the kitchen and snaking in through the gap under the door. She took the roll she'd saved and ate it, imagining a bowl of mutton broth to dip it in and Sara and Ez for company. She wondered if Sara was thinking of her, wondered if she'd even noticed what had happened. If the apothecary's boy from Lisle Street had noticed Sara then it was unlikely that Sara had noticed anything else. And as for Ez, he'd have enough worries of his own with finding a bed and something to eat without thinking of her as well. Hero sighed and chewed up the last of the bread.

The sky had faded to a strong deep blue, with a yellow orange fringe of light over Westminster. Just about now, at home, the pub would start getting busy. It was a well known ken, The Feathers. Old fighters, old trainers who had nothing to do but nurse their wounds and tell their tales would slope in around supper time and spend any money they had on beer, not food. Hero was so used to old men with broken noses and cauliflower ears she used to imagine that they were regular afflictions brought on by old age. Later, after the theatres closed, was when the young swells descended to drink and play cards and Pa would pay Sara's older brother Ned to play the fiddle. The Feathers was the best inn in all London for the followers of the fancy. Everyone knew that.

When she was younger, Hero liked the young men with plenty of money and beautiful leather boots; they would tell her jokes and bring her toffees. But they looked at her differently now, and she didn't like it.

'Oi, you! Wake up!'

Daniel careered in through the window. He was wearing a dark jacket, 'One for you, too, it's fairly cold,' and carrying a bag over his shoulder. Hero smelt the jacket first and wondered who had worn it before. Then she stood up and brushed the crumbs from her dress. She pulled the hem up and tied it around her middle so her thin legs stuck out like brown twigs at the bottom. Daniel tried not to laugh. Hero pretended not to notice, but she reminded herself to get him later.

Hero watched Daniel spit on his hands and jump up onto the windowsill. He stood up and, holding tight on to the window frame, reached with his leg to where the roof dipped. His toes made it but a loose piece of brick skittered down into the street below and Hero turned away.

'See, done it,' Daniel called out from the roof. 'What you mustn't do is look down. Then it's a piece of cake.'

Hero spat on her hands and rubbed them together. She put one foot on to the sill and climbed up. She gritted her teeth and dug her hands into the window frame.

'Come on, Hero, you can do it.'

She shut her eyes and reached across with her leg. It felt in the air and found nothing for what seemed like ages. She felt the wood of the window frames splintering in her hands and made one last effort.

'Done it!'

The flat part of the roof was narrow, really just a large

gutter between the V of the tiled part that sloped up on either side. Hero leant against the tiles. 'What do we do now?'

'Look.' Daniel pointed south to the river. In the dark London looked like fairyland—strings of lights then nothing. Pitch darkness—noises everywhere, people moving but hidden. Hero loved it, the whole city. Sara often talked about a fine house in the country, at Highgate or Hackney, but Hero knew she never wanted to be anywhere else.

'We're going that way.' Daniel pointed into the dark towards the river. The light from a boat glided eerily along in the dark, like a spectre in a ghost story. Hero thought of the spirits of hanged men roaming around that the old fighters in The Feathers used to frighten her with.

'Hero! Come on!' Daniel was already over next door and heading for the bakery at the end of White Kennet Street. Hero followed. At least in the dark it was easier to kid yourself the ground wasn't so far away. At the end of the street Daniel had found a way down. It was tricky as the bakers were still up. Arguing about who would be on earlies the next day. Hero could see them through the window, a flickering candle changing the shape of their red faces and white hands. They stabbed the air with pointing fingers at each other. Carefully Hero slid down the guttering onto the back extension and jumped into the back courtyard where Daniel was waiting. The ground felt good underneath her feet and they both ran all the way across Camomile Street towards the river.

Hero felt free. There were still enough people about in and out of the dark streets. Small sinewy link boys shepherding customers through the courts of the Minories. A blaze of light as they rounded a corner then darker still after they'd gone. Soon Hero could smell the river, not just the dirty water, but the smells of a thousand ships from all around the world, spices, coffee, tea, and leather.

Every time they passed an inn with the noise and the fug of ale and tobacco smoke Hero felt a wave of homesickness. Knots of girls—younger, older, Hero didn't know—drifted through the city streets in see-through muslin dresses, giggling and shouting.

'Oi! Oi! Oi!' Three of them cornered Daniel, grinning. As they came closer Hero could see their faces were streaks of make-up. Red lips, blue eyes, pink cheeks, white foreheads. They looked like wraiths or banshees or perhaps they were the spirits of people cut down at Tyburn or Upminster.

'Little Jew boy, little Jew boy.' They weren't wraiths, they were children. 'Got any money, little Jew boy? Want some fun?' Daniel was nearly terrified.

'They're just teasing.' Hero shooed them away and the three girls wisped off into the dark after a band of soldiers just off a boat from Belgium.

They walked on until the narrow lane opened out, but if anything it seemed darker. Hero slowed and Daniel did too. He tugged her back. 'It's Tower Hill.'

In front of them a massive dark squat shape blocked the space between them and the river. Hero could hear the water now, a greasy slooshing above the noise of the night city. She could even see in the dark the fingers of masts and imagined the sound of the wood and sail creaking. Like in the dream.

'Are you cold?' Daniel whispered. 'You shivered.'

'It's nothing. Why are you whispering?'

'I think it's the Tower, it's terrifying, in the dark.'

Hero nodded. More than that though; terrible, like something out of the Old Testament.

'Which way?'

'Well, I asked around at school and we just have to try the quays between here and London Bridge.'

They crept past the Tower. It looked almost alive and ready to spring up off its fat haunches and suffocate them with its bulk. Round past the fish market, the cobbles slippery with old slime, and down to the water's edge. The hulks of the great wooden boats rocked and moved like dreaming sleepers.

'So what do we do now, schoolboy? Ring the bell and enquire within? Maybe look for the sign that says slaves bought and sold?'

'Hero, I'm thinking!'

In the end they went from ship to ship. No one had seen anything. Some sailors spat at them, others were nice as pie. Some sailors tried to buy Daniel, some wanted Hero. It was past midnight and Daniel was getting twitchy.

'Listen, if anyone at home finds I've gone I'm as good as dead.'

'Just one more boat, Dan, please?'

'Hero, we've tried everything. He must have sailed from Westminster or downriver, or someone here would've known. Let's go home. Please?'

Hero sighed. Daniel was right. Her legs ached from walking and she was hungry again.

'Got any cash, Dan?'

Daniel had twopence.

'Enough for a pie,' Hero said.

'But everywhere's shut!'

'There's not.' Hero pointed into a court off the quay. There was a thin yellow light from around the door and the sound of voices.

'Come on, Hero, I'm not going in there!'

'But I'm starving! My stomach's so empty I could swallow a horse and still have room for another! Come with me? Please?'

They walked up to the door and pushed it open. Inside three rush candles flickered around the room. Every movement made the shadows jump on the walls. There were around fifteen men, the sort Pa never let in The Feathers unless he knew them very well. Bristly or bearded, faces creased like leather that had been wet and dry and wet and dry. Long clay pipes jammed into mouths. There was a man behind a huge wooden table. A big man, his head seemed to graze the ceiling.

'Garn! Off with you, twinkies. It's time your mammy put you in your beds. Clear off with you now!'

Hero smiled nervously. Daniel hissed at her. 'I don't reckon they've got any food. Let's go.'

Hero thought. If anyone in the whole of London was going to be kidnapping Pa it would be one of these men. She had to ask. It was perfect. She made her way to the big man. She swallowed to clear her throat and asked clearly and loudly.

'Excuse me!' Twenty-nine eyes swivelled her way. 'I was wondering if any of you gentlemen (some laughter here) had seen or heard of my father? John da Costa, the fighter.' She scanned the room. There was silence for what seemed like ages then the big man broke into a black-toothed grin.

'John da Costa! The Dark Destroyer, your father! Well I never!'

He clapped her on the back and Hero nearly fell over. 'John da Costa! One of the finest niggers that ever walked. Of course! Why I never saw it, looking at you! Sit down, sit down! Coffee!' The men grinned with approval and a few came up to shake Hero's hand. She had to wipe it in the folds of her dress afterwards. Daniel was grinning.

'What did I say about your pa, Hero? What did I say! A treasure!'

They sat Hero and Dan down and put half a round loaf and a meat pie on the table along with two filthy mugs of ale.

'On the house!' The drinkers to a man swore they'd heard nothing at the docks and promised they'd keep an eye out for her sake.

Hero chewed the pie even though it was hard as a stone and tucked the loaf inside her jacket.

'We have to go, Hero! It'll be getting light before long.'

Hero nodded, and they said goodbye and shook more hands over and over again and made their way along the quay.

There was a shout from above and a small boy, shorter than Daniel, monkeyed down a rope from the ship and jumped onto the quayside beside them. It won't hurt to ask one more time, Hero thought.

'Hello.' Hero spoke slowly and loudly at him in case he spoke no English. 'We're looking for a man, a man,' she stood on tiptoes and stretched her arm up, 'this tall. Big man. Black hair, dark eyes.'

'A Negro, we're looking for a Negro, kidnapped, yesterday,' Dan added. The boy grinned and Hero had to stop herself gasping. His teeth had been filed into little points.

'A Negro? Which one? There's hundreds working ships all along by the river.' The boy spoke perfect English.

'John da Costa.'

'The pugilist,' Daniel said.

'He means boxer.'

The boy shrugged. 'There's rules about kidnapping. But no one takes no notice. I was taken so long ago I can't remember my own mother.'

'Piet!' A loud deep shout made the boy jump and climb back up the rope as quickly as he'd made it down.

Hero sighed. Dan hurried homewards along the quay and she followed him. Pa could be anywhere. There were so many boats and so many people. In the dark all the ships were like huge wooden beasts. In dock they stood high in the water and Hero looked up at the massive wooden walls and imagined Pa just on the other side. Chained up with a hundred others just like in the dream. Of course the English trade had been stopped—in theory at least—three years ago. But slaves were still shipped from Africa to the plantations of Brazil and America, and there were more than a few English sea captains who would turn a blind eye to carrying slaves if the price was right.

Perhaps if she shouted as loud as she could he would hear her. Hero stopped where the crowd of boats was thickest and yelled, 'John da Costa! John da Costa!' Her voice bounced off the stone buildings of the quayside then buried itself in the sides of the ships. Nothing happened. She read the names of the boats, beautiful, hopeful names, some outlined in shiny gold leaf: the *Maid of Heaven*, the *Phoenicia*, the *Golden Venture*, the *Hibiscus*. They told her nothing.

'Hero, let's go.' Daniel called to her from a flight of broad steps that led back up to the city. 'I can come back in the morning.'

Hero looked at the ships rocking softly on the water. They looked too big to float. They ought to sink.

'Come on.'

Hero turned too. They were both exhausted and the gentle slope up from the river seemed mountainous. St Paul's chimed two o'clock as Hero and Dan trudged home.

'It'll work out, Hero. I promise. If he had sailed someone would know, one of those old sailors, they'd have told us. We'll find him. Tomorrow at synagogue I'll ask Ikey and George to come with me and we'll sort it, Hero, we will. Ikey's dad does ship brokering—he knows what goes on and comes off every boat that leaves the Pool.' Dan was getting excited thinking about it. 'Then me an' them'll come down here, with Ikey's big brother and—'

'Daniel, you don't understand. This isn't just a game. This is everything. If I can't get Pa back my life is ruined. What if he is on a ship?'

They walked on in silence.

They were within spitting distance of the Houndsditch when an echo of shouts behind them stopped them in their tracks. 'Da Costa! Da Costa!'

Hero and Dan swivelled round. Three men were running up the lane behind them. The one in front had an old-fashioned army coat that spread out behind him as he ran. They didn't look friendly, they looked scary. But they might just know something. She stopped.

'Yes?'

Dan stopped too.

'You're looking for da Costa, the nigger?'

The men stopped running and started walking slowly, their boots heavy on the cobbled street. Hero nodded.

'What's he to you then, girly? Your pa, is it?'

Daniel tugged at her. 'Hero, we've got to go. These blokes aren't friendly.' He kept his voice low. The men were coming nearer all the time, and the nearer they got, the larger they seemed to grow. Their slow swaggering walk made them fill up all the narrow lane.

One of them pulled off his scarf and began winding it around his fists. Hero knew she ought to run, but if they knew, if they really knew where Pa was . . .

She held her voice steady. 'Where is he, then?'

'Well.' The largest man grinned. 'We've got a message from Mr da Costa.' The men walked closer. Hero felt her insides turn over. She knew it was a trick, she knew they were lying but she couldn't stop herself.

'Pa? You've seen him?'

'We've seen him all right, haven't we, boys? He says, he's going home and you can come with him if you like, girly.'

'Hero, it's a trick, it's a trick.' Daniel was whispering now. He had pulled his jacket tight and turned up the collar. 'I know who they are! Come on.' He pulled her away and she saw his eyes. He was terrified. They broke into a run.

At the same moment the three men ran too, big hard strides coming closer over the cobbles. Daniel was quick. He darted in and out of courts and lanes. Hero had longer legs but it was hard to keep up. Still the men were gaining on them.

'We have to hide, Dan, I can't run any more!' Hero's legs felt like ribbons of toffee and she couldn't breathe.

'You've got to! Come on!' Daniel hissed. 'Those men, those men work for—' Hero didn't hear him finish his sentence as he rounded another corner and they were in front of the baker's at the corner of White Kennet Street. Hero could feel the warmth of the ovens and smell the yeasty smell of raw bread.

Looking up she could see Daniel had already pulled himself up onto the low roof. Hero tried jumping up, but the men were closer, she could hear them.

'Quick! Hide!' Daniel pointed at the sacks of flour in the baker's yard. Hero jumped down amongst them and crouched in between the flour. They heard the men's footsteps come closer, slow to a walk, then stop.

'Can't see 'em, John.' The men were breathless too.

'Where've they gone then, back to the Silvers?'

'By the looks of it.'

'I'll see the old bird in the morning. I reckon we've scared them enough for a night.'

They know! Hero thought. They know where I'm staying! They know who I am!

The baker came out into the yard and filled his clay pipe. He leant on the wall and tried lighting his pipe from a tinder box he took out of his grey-white apron. Hero shifted. Her leg was squashed underneath her body and now it felt like a rat was nibbling through the cloth of her shoe.

She brushed her foot. The large brown rat that had been nibbling happily on the cloth of her shoe squeaked and Hero, covered in best Hampshire flour, jumped a foot into the air.

The baker, sucking hard on his pipe, sucked too hard and swallowed his tobacco. The next morning, when his brother woke to fire up the ovens, he told him he'd seen the ghost of that Lascar's daughter they'd poisoned two years ago, and swore never to cut the flour with talc or lime again.

By the time Hero had made it up to the roof Daniel had gone. He must have got tired waiting, Hero thought. He wasn't in her room when she slid back through the open window. He must have gone to his bed. But he had said—she could have sworn it—that he knew who those men were.

Hero didn't fancy inching round the front of the Silvers' house on the dodgy parapet. She pulled one boot off. She should ask now, get the whole thing clear in her mind. She lay back on the bed. She was exhausted. Daniel would be around in the morning. He'd probably come whistling through the window before synagogue. Hero was so tired she was asleep before she'd taken the other boot off.

FIVE

Hero must have been dreaming about The Feathers. There was the incredible loud banging and tearing and creaking sound as the mahogany doors were kicked in by the magistrate's men and Hero sat upright in the bed. She blinked, taking in the bare plaster walls of the little bedroom at the top of the Silvers' house. She wasn't at home. She calmed herself, waited until her heart had stopped pounding from the dream and swung her legs out of bed. Suddenly the door banged open and Hero jumped with shock. Mrs Silver swished into the room, her yellow and purple face livid in the bright sunlight.

'Hero da Costa! Hero da Costa!' Aunt Silver poked her with the end of the yard broom. She had it held out in front of herself for protection. Hero thought this must be part of the dream. Rachel stood behind her mother grinning. She was wearing her Saturday best, and Lily Juliet's wedding slippers.

'I know what you've been up to, you lying undeserving wretch!'

Hero felt the end of the broom digging into her ribs. It was too painful to be anything other than reality. Aunt Silver walked crabwise around the bed, kicking at the flour-stained jacket Hero had thrown on the floor last night. The loaf skittered out and hit the skirting.

'See! See! You've been out, haven't you! Out all night I'll warrant, consorting with the night and all his demons!'

Rachel smirked. Aunt Silver pinned Hero to the wall with the broom.

'It's for your own good. You act like an animal and I'll treat you like one.'

How did Aunt Silver know? Did Daniel tell her, had he set her up? Hero opened her mouth to speak but Aunt Silver got in first.

'You were seen, girl! Seen out at midnight by the docks looking for your nigger father! That potwipe of a tavern boy by your side. Ungrateful bitch! If you think you're staying in my house one minute longer, you've got another think coming! Rachel! Fetch the men! Now!'

Hero couldn't move with the broom handle pressing into her chest. She could hardly breathe and Aunt Silver's bruised face was like a ha'penny horror mask; she looked like a severed head in floral starched linen.

She could hear the steps of two or three people coming upstairs, hard heavy boots, big tall men.

'I was just looking for Pa!' There was no point in lying. 'I didn't do anything else, Aunt, honest.' Aunt Silver's face was frozen with rage.

'Aunt! Too late for buttering me up now. I'm decided.'

With that three men pushed through into the bedroom. Hero looked from her aunt's face to the three smiling brown-haired men. They smiled broadly at her, the biggest one showing no teeth.

'Hello again, girly.'

Hero could feel herself sweating. She'd seen him before. She'd seen all of them before. It was the same men that had come with the cart to The Feathers. The same men that had loaded up the furniture and carted it off. The same men that had dropped Pa's best gilt mirror into a thousand shiny pieces in the gutter. And it was the same men that had chased her and Daniel all the way home last night.

Hero fainted. When she woke, Mrs Isaacs the cook was pressing a wet rag to her lips. She couldn't ever remember fainting before. She tried to remember the sinking feeling, like dissolving salt in water. Mrs Isaacs saw that she was awake and brought her a small cup. Hero reached up for it and found that her hands had been tied together with an old belt. She looked down. They'd tied her feet too.

'There there, child, it's for the best.' Mrs Isaacs mopped her brow. 'I know you're a strong girl and everyone else is off at synagogue so it's just you and me.'

Hero looked from the woman's kindly face to her strap-bound hands. It had to be a joke. This really couldn't be happening. Maybe they were going to sell her after all. Sell her and ship her off.

'Will they sell me?'

'Heavens no, child! The Silvers are good people. The master says you're going to work in his new warehouse. There now, things will all turn out fine. You've just got to learn to control that terrible temper! Mrs Silver says you can't be helping it, what with it being in your blood an' all.'

'But, Mrs Isaacs, you know me, I'm Hero da Costa, I'm their niece. I'm not an animal.'

'Don't you fret, dearie. I think you're really rather pretty, if dingy, when you're not sulking, that is. Now, don't you move, I'm off to the yard a minute.' And she bustled out of the kitchen.

Hero bit at the belt that cut into her wrists but it was too thick and she just hurt her teeth. She tried standing up, wriggling like a caterpillar and then leaning against the wall, but she fell over twice, the second time her head hit the floor hard.

She could do nothing. Her nose hurt and her cheek felt skinned. Powerless. If someone had told her yesterday that life could get any worse she'd have doubted them. But now here she was rolling around on the blackened sticky floor of the Silvers' scullery bound hand and foot. She pulled herself sitting again as she heard the yard door bang.

'Lovely day outside, it is, chicken.'

Hero shut her eyes so she wouldn't cry.

She sat there all day. She heard the family return and she hoped Dan would come down, he'd help her out surely. But he didn't come. At supper time Mrs Isaacs let her have the left overs and an extra dumpling because she felt sorry for her but she wouldn't loosen the belt around Hero's wrists, even though she asked.

.

It was after dark when Tyndall, the big man with no teeth, came for her. Hero thought he was taking her to the ship where they said Pa was. 'Shame, much as my companions and myself would appreciate a pretty passenger like yourself, it's Mr Silver's new warehouse you're going to.'

Uncle Silver's rag warehouse was not far, a short walk beyond the new church and the other side of Spitalfields. Tyndall had stuffed an old piece of rag into her mouth so she couldn't yell; Hero tried not to retch when she tasted his snot in her mouth. She hoped it was only snot. It was dark and the tall, old silk weavers' houses looked dirty and tired, but there were plenty of tiny alleyways and dark courts she could run into. If only she could free herself. The man marched her along holding her right arm behind her in an armlock, twisting it tighter if Hero so much as slackened her step. Hero could see up ahead that the road was widening out and that this would be her last chance. With her free hand she elbowed him where it hurt most.

'No wonder as they wants rid of you!' The man laughed. 'For a woman, not a growed woman even, you're strong. Not as strong as me though, eh?' And he twisted Hero's arm tighter until she thought it would break. 'Still, no wonder what with your family. John da Costa! I never saw him fight meself, I was working then, on the boats, Bridgetown, London, Havana, London. The name's Tyndall, by the way.'

Hero stopped listening. The man droned on and on about fighting and Hero wished she hadn't been born a girl. If she'd been a boy, Grandpa would have taught her everything, trained her up properly and she'd be earning good money in the ring. And she'd be able to knock this Tyndall out easy.

He yanked her round a corner, 'Here we go,' and rattled a huge bunch of keys out of his jacket with his free hand. There were large wooden double doors, big enough for carts and a smaller door cut into one for people. He pushed Hero ahead of him into the building. There was a small cobbled, uncovered yard and another door beyond that. The man didn't let go of her until he'd locked the outer door. He threw her off and Hero had to stop herself from landing on the ground. She pulled the gag out of her mouth.

'Right.' He jangled the keys again. 'Mr Silver says there's a room what should do for you through here.' He unlocked the second door. The man opened it and grinned at her. Hero could tell he was grinning from the shape his eyes made in his now screwed-up face. Hero didn't move.

'Come on, get yerself inside, I got other things to be doing tonight.' She could try screaming before he got too close. Hero gulped in a deep breath of air. Then she screamed.

'That's it!' Tyndall lunged forward and cupped his hand around her mouth. He was right in her face now. She could smell the gin on his breath, see the three teeth left at the back of his mouth. He pressed her against the wall so she couldn't move.

'Clever? I don't think so. How old are you, girl?' Hero felt his leg push between hers. 'Let's go inside shall we, see your new home.' He smiled at her, a poisonous smile. Hero was terrified. She knew if she didn't do something soon something terrible would happen.

Inside the warehouse were trestle tables piled with clothes. The smells of all the hundreds of people who had worn these thousands of clothes without thinking of washing hung in the air. Tyndall kept hold of her with one hand as he locked the door. Hero tried to see a way out through the darkness. Tyndall dropped the bunch of keys and let go of her for an instant. Hero ran off at a sprint then ducked under a table and crawled away. She crouched, making herself as small as she could, listening as he walked up and down in the dark warehouse. But he didn't find her.

'I haven't got time for games, girl!' he shouted into the dark at her. 'You might think you're safe now, but I know where you are. And I think my friends would like to meet you too.'

Hero curled herself tighter. She listened as she heard Tyndall let himself out and lock the door after him. She listened as he crossed the courtyard and slammed the little wooden door. She stayed where she was, as she was, and didn't even realize she'd fallen asleep until it was already morning.

'You should have put her in the office, I gave you instructions!' It was her uncle's voice that woke her up.

'Yessir.' And that was Tyndall's. 'But she was vicious. Elbowed me, she did.'

'Quite. If I thought that twelve-year-old girls were that much of a hindrance I wouldn't have hired you.'

'Yessir.'

'Hero!' Mr Silver shouted for her. 'Hero! Come out at once!'

Hero ached all over. She must have slept all night in a tight ball. Her arms were numb and her neck cricked. She thought about not coming out but it was light now and they'd find her soon enough.

'Are you sure the girl's still here? If you've lost her the deal's off. With da Costa still in the compter we're not out of the woods yet.'

Hero listened. Da Costa. He meant Pa! She almost shouted with joy.

'If you please, sir.'

'Hmm?'

'We sails next week; I can't do anything about that, sir. If your man's not ready, the boat goes, with or without da Costa, and our Mr Owen in Bridgetown won't wait forever.'

'Quite! Quite! Can you not bother me with that now, Tyndall. It seems you cannot subdue a twelve-year-old girl, so how on earth will you manage when I deliver you a grown man and a fighter at that?'

'The girl's here, sir!' Tyndall had spied her. Hero stepped out and stood up slowly, uncurling herself. As Tyndall approached Hero backed off. She made for where her uncle was standing. He was, at least, the sort who wouldn't hurt you himself, but didn't mind paying someone else to do the hurting.

'Ah! There you are!'

Hero said nothing. She was trying to look as though she wasn't scared of Tyndall, to hold the expression frozen on her face so they couldn't see what she was thinking or feeling.

'Yes, Hero. We'll have you working in here with the other girls.'

He motioned to Tyndall who took her arm and led her to a bench at the side of one of the tables. Hero tried not to think about the way Tyndall's thick fingers cut into her arm. She longed to speak, to ask what a compter was, did he mean counter, did he mean country? Behind her blank face her mind was racing.

'A bit of work will probably do you the world of good, stop you sitting around moping about what may or may not have happened, yes?'

Tyndall sat her down and Mr Silver passed him a hessian sack. Inside it Hero could hear a chain, the same noise as the dream.

Tyndall pulled out a leg iron.

'Fix it on, will you, my man.' Mr Silver looked back

to Hero. 'I am most sorry about this, but you've shown over the past few days that you really can't be trusted. Hmm?'

Hero said nothing. She stared at one brick on the far wall and held her face still. Compter Counter Country Comply Complete Complain.

'Bit of honest work, mixing with other girls your age. You show me that you can be good, we'll see what I can do. Yes?'

Hero said nothing.

He chucked her under the chin. 'Buck up, girl, buck up. You show me what you can do, eh?' He smiled. 'And don't worry yourself, it's all completely above the law. You're to work for me until you're twenty-one and I give you food and lodgings. The papers will be drawn up today and you can sign them for me tomorrow. You can write your name at least, can't you?'

'But that's slavery!' The words burst out of her.

'No, no, no! Indentured labour! After all, if I'm to feed and clothe you it's only right that I'm reimbursed, hmm?' He pulled out his pocket watch. 'The girls come in around eight. In the meantime you can thank Mrs Isaacs for this.' He pulled out a loaf and a flask from a canvas bag.

Tyndall closed the iron cuff around Hero's ankle and locked the chain to the bench. Hero sat still.

'There you go, sir.' He handed Mr Silver the key. Mr Silver looked into Hero's blank face and rolled his eyes.

'Look at that, Tyndall.' Mr Silver clicked his fingers under Hero's nose. She didn't flinch. 'That is Negro insolence. I've read about it, oh yes! Still, work will soon wear that one down, there has to be some good in her. Oh, and Tyndall, fetch her a bucket, so she doesn't mess the floor.'

Hero didn't move as they walked away.

When she was quite sure they'd gone she tugged and pulled and wrestled with the leg-iron but it made no difference. Outside she could hear church bells, and people, but far off. They wouldn't hear her whatever noise she made. She made a hollow in the pile of old clothes in front of her and put her head down. Uncle Silver had said da Costa was still in the compter. Daniel would know what that meant. For once Hero wished she knew about things. Read things instead of just hit things. Compter? Where was Daniel now she needed him? Did he even know where she was? Maybe everyone had forgotten her, Dan and Sara and Ez. Just like that. She almost started crying. Pulled her hands up to her face and felt the iron cutting into her leg. Hero stopped herself. She would never forget about Pa. She would never stop looking. Crying was a waste of time.

SIX

Hero had exhausted herself with tugging and pulling at the chain. She managed to wear away some of the table prop but it would be forever before she broke it through. Her hands ached and smelt of iron, and her only blue dress was now more tatty than the piles of rags in front of her. Then she heard the girls arrive. She heard the sound of the outer doors opening and she heard wooden shoes crossing the stone yard. Hero watched them come in, eight of them, not all girls, two younger, two around the same age, the others older. One had a baby strapped to her front, one was old, walked with a stick, and had a head of grey frothy hair under an old-fashioned tie bonnet. She moved as if she had no feet, gliding, rustling along in her skirts, swishing up the dust on the floor.

They all stared at Hero as if she were an animal in a menagerie or an exhibit at the fair. Their eyes flicked up and down from her face to the chain. Face. Chain. Face. The younger girls elbowed each other and giggled.

The old woman brought her stick down hard on a table and the pile of clothes jumped an inch into the air.

'Right!' The little ones scurried to their places. The older girls sighed and the mother jiggled her baby to quieten it.

'Mister Silver has explained the situation to me, and I will tell you girls what you need to know and no more. This is a place of work, and work is what I expect of you, from all of you.' She looked at Hero. 'So! No more jawing than usual.' The old woman sat down and Hero was surprised to see her tiny wooden shoes sticking out like dolls' feet from under her skirts. 'This here new girl,' she pointed with her stick, 'is to be working with us for a while. You're all to treat her as if she's hardly here, don't go swapping life stories, and don't go asking her no questions. And you, madam, don't go answering them. The leg-iron's for her own and our safety, Mister Silver says, and we're to leave it be. And lastly, and most important, Mister Silver says as if we wants to keep our jobs we don't go telling anyone she's here.' The woman looked hard at all the girls around the room. 'Got that? Good!'

In two seconds every girl was sitting down and clothes were almost flying this way and that into different sacks. The old woman glided across to Hero.

'Right,' she said and heaved herself down onto the bench. 'I don't know what it is you've done.' She raised her hand to stop Hero from speaking. 'Right or wrong, good or bad, makes no difference to me.' Hero sighed and stared down at the floor where a trail of mouse droppings led away under the table. 'I'm in charge here, remember that. And if I've no job, then I don't eat, and I don't have nowhere to live.' Hero thought that it wouldn't matter if the old woman didn't eat for a week from the size of her. 'So. I know which side I'm on and it ain't yours. That said I'm a fair woman, treat me fair and I'll treat you fair. The name's French, Mrs French. Though I've never set foot beyond Deptford.' The woman smiled, spat on her hand and held it out for Hero to shake. Hero didn't move. 'Truth is,' Mrs French went on, 'we've all of us had bad times, really bad times, and if we're lucky we nearly all comes out the other side.' Mrs French's hand hung in space.

Hero looked at it, looked at her sun-browned and wrinkled skin loose on her face. Hero did nothing. 'Ah well, I can see your point.' The old woman rubbed her hand dry on her skirts. 'But there's no use in you and me not being civil.'

Hero said nothing.

'Well, I'll get Debsey to show you the ropes.' The old woman hauled herself up with her stick. 'Debsey!'

A small girl with sunken-in cheeks, as if she had held her breath and couldn't let it out again, jumped at the mention of her name.

'Come here and show Hero what's what.'

Debsey shuffled over. Hero could see as she got nearer that her mousy hair was grey with lice, and she was glad when Debsey didn't come too close. Debsey smiled.

'See, you go through this lot.' She pulled out a pair of canvas breeches that stank as high as the bucket Tyndall had left her. 'These go for rags.' She threw them behind her into the correct pile without even looking. 'And this . . . ' It was a velvet bodice, old-fashioned, so worn it was bald, but you could still see the bright flashes of emerald green in the seams. It made Hero think of the dancing girls in Berwick Street. 'This goes for sale. But these,' she pulled out a pair of hardly worn light cotton drawers, 'anything on the tasty side like this, Silver sells to some shop up west.'

Hero looked down at her own dress. It was streaked with dirt and torn from clambering over the roofs. She didn't look any different from any of the other sifting girls.

''Sall right here, really!' Debsey tried to cheer her up. 'You'll get used to it. 'Sbetter than weaving, a hundred times better. Not to mention straw plaiting or making buttons. I had a sister once, lost both her thumbs making horn buttons!'

Hero tried to smile back.

'Listen.' Debsey put her head nearer Hero's. Hero moved back. 'How did you get that thing on your leg? My mate Ems says you killed a man!'

'Come on, ladies!' Mrs French thumped her stick again. 'This ain't no Quarter Fair!'

Debsey shuffled back to her place. Hero started through her pile. She had to look to check the clothes she was sorting were going in the right place, but it was easy after a while.

She thought of all the people who must have worn these clothes. There were cloaks, and waistcoats with half the embroidery rubbed off, a single white kid glove which did up with tiny buttons. Hero wondered where the other one was: lying behind the sofa in a west end salon.

They stopped for bread and ale at noon. Hero watched the other girls as they walked around; she envied them stretching their legs, imagined running and dancing.

No one spoke to her. She asked Mrs French when they went home and she just said when it got dark. Hero hoped that Tyndall and his men would have something else to do tonight.

One of the big girls, Essie or Lina, Hero had heard their names, complained about the smell of Hero's bucket.

'It's like a byre in here, Mrs French!'

'Then you'll feel right at home, ducky,' Mrs French smiled back.

Hero watched Debsey ask for leave to go home to feed her little brother. She felt a breeze as the door opened and watched as Debsey slipped away and heard the noises of the Sunday market in the street. If only it could be that simple for her. The mother walked between the tables singing to her baby. It was a boy; she called him George, like the king.

Mrs French sat like a jailer between her and the others, and it wasn't until later, when Debsey had returned and everyone was hard at it again that Mrs French moved.

Since she'd come back Debsey had been staring right at Hero; she didn't even bother looking away when Hero stared back.

'I'm going for me snifter,' Mrs French said and glided out. There was quiet until they heard the outer door slam and the girls slowed down their work and then stopped completely.

Hero saw Debsey standing on tiptoes, looking out of the high windows to check that she'd gone. She was about to say something when one of the older girls shouted at Hero.

''Ere!' It was the one called Essie. ''Ere, Lina says you're related to the boss.'

Hero didn't answer at first, she was still trying to work out what Debsey was up to. Something, she was sure of it.

''Ere, cloth ears!' The girl stood up.

'What?'

'You! Hero da Whatsit, are you related to Silver?'

'What if I am?'

'Don't treat his kin too good, that's all I'm saying.'

'It's 'cause she's a touch sooty, if you get my meaning, Essie.' Lina nudged her friend.

'Are you his girl, then? Are you? Wrong side of the sheets an' all?'

Hero was furious. 'He's never my pa in a million years! My pa's been nabbed and locked up 'cause of him, taken everything we've got and he's supposed to be my uncle! He's no more my family now . . . than, than you lot!'

'Oo-oh, angry, aren't we!' Lina was grinning.

Debsey and her little friend Ems had been listening wide eyed.

'What you done then? To be chained up like that?' Essie asked.

Hero was still red faced. 'I "done" nothing, see?'

'All right, all right.'

'Leave her alone, you!' Debsey stood up on the table. 'I know who she is and everything. They've all got it in for her, young master told me.'

The girl with the baby shifted the wriggling boy in her lap. 'Since when does anyone that wears proper shoes talk to you when they don't have to?'

Debsey flushed. She had promised the young master she wouldn't tell.

'Do you mean Daniel?' Hero asked.

'Young Mister Silver.' Debsey whispered it.

Essie and Lina crossed the room and sat down either side of Hero. Lina bent down and rattled the chain,

47

jerking Hero's leg. Hero knew she could knock them both out but she couldn't get away.

'Mrs French is coming!' Debsey piped up and Lina and Essie were back at their places in seconds and sorting clothes as if their lives depended on it.

After a few minutes Mrs French didn't appear. Lina got angry and made to wallop Debsey but the woman with the baby stopped her.

'You two're worse than a pair of idle boys. Nothing to do but tease that poor girl and now hitting Debsey? Ain't you ever knowed any darkies? They get the sharp end of any stick and that's the truth. If they're honest or not, it's always the same. And you should know, "Daughters of Israel" and all!' She shook her head.

Lina and Essie pretended not to notice.

'There's some'd put all of us in the same boat and drown us together!'

Hero smiled thank you at the mother, and slowly everyone started settling back to their places. Hero strained to see through the window if the yard was clear. She shut her ears to the chatter of the girls and when she was quite sure she couldn't hear Mrs French's clogs she called to Debsey.

'Debsey!'

'Yes?' Debsey looked round and shuffled nearer.

'Thanks for that. I'd have put their lights out if I hadn't been chained up. Listen, did you really see Dan Silver out there? What did he say?'

'He asked if you were here an' I told him an' that. Said as how they'd chained you up. He gave me this.' She passed Hero a scrap of paper. Hero opened it on her lap and stared at Daniel's spidery writing. It took some time for her to make sense of it.

See you tonight, it said. *Don't worry, Daniel.*

Don't worry. Thanks for nothing, Hero thought, what if Tyndall gets here first. But then at least Daniel hadn't forgotten her.

Debsey was still sitting next to her on the bench, grinning.

'Thank you, Debsey.'

' 'Sall right.' Debsey blushed.

Hero looked at her. She was nine or ten, thin as a yard broom, and her face was dirty as her dress. There was a cleaner patch in the middle around her nose and mouth were she'd wiped it and Hero thought of the life she'd had before. Two cotton dresses, a pair of shoes, and as much food as a girl could eat. If she ever got home, got her life back, she'd take Ez up Berwick Street market and buy him a pair too. She imagined him cramming his hard as nails feet into a pair of soft leather shoes and smiled.

Pa. She must keep thinking about Pa. Debsey got up off the bench and jumped down. Debsey's face wasn't a nine-year-old's face. It was the face of a woman who had seen everything. Hero liked to think there was nothing she didn't know about. She'd seen Lord Camelford sitting in the back bar at The Feathers with three women the night before his wedding and none of them was his future wife. But she didn't know what a compter was.

'Debsey, wait.'

'Mmm?'

Hero felt foolish asking, but you never know, she thought, it's always worth a try.

'Do you know what a compter is?'

'Compter? Like at Poultry or Southwark?'

Hero felt her heart start racing. She knew. This little strip of lice ridden girl knew.

'I don't know, that's why I'm asking!'

'No need to get shirty with me.' Debsey felt a little scared. This girl was chained up; who knows what she might do.

'Debsey, Debsey, sorry. I'm sorry.' Hero tried to keep herself calm. 'Look, I don't know, I really just don't know.'

Two woollen skirts, stiff with grease, flew over Debsey's head. She grinned now; happy, for once in her life, to be knowledgeable.

'It's like a lock-up, you know, like jail?'

'A lock-up!' Hero knew about lock-ups. The Soho parish lock-up was full of drunks usually, and boys who thieved for a living. 'A lock-up!'

'Yes.'

'And where's the Poultry compter, Debsey, do you know that?'

'Well now, Poultry compter's in the Poultry, and Southwark compter's over the river and I never been there. But Poultry compter's in the City. I know that see, 'cause that's where my ma went last Whitsun when they said she'd been nobbling punters over Bishopsgate.' Debsey scuttled back to her place as Mrs French crossed the yard.

'If you see Daniel outside, tell him to come quick!' Hero called after her.

The afternoon sped by. Hero threw the clothes she was supposed to be sorting anyhow. Pa was in a lock-up, and he could still take care of himself, Hero thought. No one but a fool would give John da Costa any trouble. Except, she thought, throwing a linen shirt onto the wrong pile, unless someone was out to prove something, a dare in prison. 'Fight the famous Dark Destroyer if you can.' She saw it all in her head. Pa would be bruised and bloody and half starved. Hero couldn't bear to think about it. She should be grateful Pa wasn't halfway around the world in the hold of a slave ship. But what if Pa thought she'd forgotten him, thought everyone had forgotten him?

Hero sighed. At least Daniel was looking out for her. But how could Daniel get her out? Maybe lard or dripping round her ankle would do it. No, that was stupid, he'd have to have the key. What if Tyndall got here first? Daniel couldn't fight them off.

Chopping her foot off seemed the only reasonable answer. But there wasn't a knife sharp enough anyway. Hero looked out of the high windows at the darkening sky. She hadn't realized that it was so late. The pile of clothes, light and dark, had taken on the same shade of grey and the girls were slowing down.

'Right, girls, off with you now.' Mrs French rattled her keys. 'See you tomorrow, Monday morning, bright and early.'

The girls vanished as quick as a magician's assistant at the pleasure gardens. Apart from a wink from Debsey no one wished her goodnight. Hero was left on her own in the dark empty room with only the sound of the mice scuttling around. At least she hoped they were mice.

SEVEN

Hero felt she was getting used to this. Whatever certainties her life had held only last week had been whipped away from under her like a dirty carpet on its way to a beating. Her life, so easy and reliable, had proved to be nothing more than a sham. A thin crust of reality that hid a snake pit. And here she was in the bottom of it. At least she knew where Pa was now. Except that she had no way of getting to him. Her sigh bounced off the lime-washed brick walls and into the depths of the piles of old clothes.

'Come on, Daniel!' she said aloud. 'This is where you're supposed to come to my rescue, unlock this thing,' she tugged on her chain, 'and get me out!'

Nothing happened.

'Please!'

She shifted on the wooden bench. Outside the new church clock rang for eight o'clock.

Hero remembered half heard conversations at The Feathers: Pa, Grandpa Reuben, a tall American, darker than Pa. They'd talk in the back room after closing—politics, the state of the fancy; one time, slavery. Hero strained to remember. Old Hero, comfortable, happy Hero da Costa, daughter and granddaughter of the licencees, would shut her ears at the mention of the word. She remembered Pa, the night before he was taken away. He'd wanted to tell her all her family history, she knew—he'd tried many many times before. She never wanted to listen. What had happened to Pa's mother, his father, his grandpa? What were they like? She could have cousins, far away, shackled just like she was now. She wished she'd listened.

She froze.

She listened now. Someone, some people, were opening the main door and crossing the yard. Outside, the light from a yellow lantern swung to and fro. She could hear two or three people; no, just two people with boots on. Tyndall, she thought, and she felt sick. They were talking, a low rumble of voices, she couldn't hear exactly what they said. She could hear the big bunch of keys jangling. Hero looked around her in the dark. The bench she was sitting on was too big and heavy to use as a weapon. The leg-iron meant she couldn't reach the broom propped up against the wall under the window. What else was there?

The key turned in the lock and the door opened. Two shadows filled the space and squeezed through at the same time. One kicked the door shut behind him but it bounced open again, flapping in the breeze.

'Hello then, girly.' Tyndall chucked her under the chin. 'Brought my friend Webster. Give him a smile like a nice girly.' Hero watched him slip the keys into his jacket.

'I hope she's nice and clean, John.' Webster was shorter than Tyndall, with a wide frog face. Hero watched him put the lantern down on the table.

'Oh, she's clean all right, Marty. Nice girl she is, from up west, better than what you're used to, an that's for sure!'

Hero waited until Webster and Tyndall were close enough.

'Bit sulky, though,' Webster said, bending forward to inspect her.

Quickly she heaved up the bucket and threw the contents into both men's faces.

'Oh my gawd!'

The two men reeled backwards, wiping the piss out of their eyes.

'Shame I didn't have the flux, eh?' Hero almost laughed.

'My Sunday jacket! My Sunday jacket! The wife'll

never be able to pop it tomorrow, not like this!' Webster took his jacket off and shook it. He knocked the lantern over and the lit candle fizzled out.

'You little nigger bitch!' Tyndall wiped his face with a rag and made to punch her.

'Not in the face! Silver won't like that!' Webster stopped him.

'I don't care what Silver likes or doesn't like!'

Hero could see the man was snarling, and she was afraid again.

'We're not supposed to be here, not now! If you want to hit her, hit her round the middle, then it won't show! That's what I do with the missus.'

Tyndall took his jacket off too. He never stopped staring at her and Hero knew it was just a matter of minutes before he started hitting her. She breathed in and out, deep and slow and clenched and unclenched her fists. They wouldn't go away unmarked, even if she was chained up.

'Right!' Tyndall drew back his fist. Hero felt it connect with her stomach before she'd had a chance to stand up and hit him. The air was forced out of her and she bent double. She flew off the bench and ended up on the floor. She would have been sent flying but the leg-iron bit into her ankle and stopped her. She had never been hit like that by anyone. She didn't feel afraid any more, only angry.

'Not so bloody quick now, are you?' Tyndall stood over her.

Hero wanted to scream but she had no breath. She knew she had to move, roll over or away, just move. But the pain in her guts was like a weight. It was hard just to open her eyes. She could feel the pain spreading out all over, she knew it would be easy to faint, or swoon. To fall into a deep, deep sleep, to feel herself dissolve, like she had done before, and then she wouldn't feel anything.

No.

She forced her eyelids apart and dug her fingernails into

her hands. Hero made herself think about that pain and not the pain in her insides. Tyndall was bending down over her. He grabbed her left shoulder and pulled her towards him. Hero could smell the spirits and the tobacco on his breath.

'Hold her, Martin!'

'I'm trying to get this lit.' Webster had the lantern open and was trying to re-light the stubby candle.

'Forget that!' Tyndall pulled Hero up.

'There!' The candle sputtered alight and the walls of the rag warehouse seemed to move as it flickered.

'There.' Webster said it again, grinning at Hero. His round face was covered in pock marks. Hero felt her strength coming back and wriggled.

'Hold her!' Tyndall was getting angry.

Webster took Hero's arm behind her in an armlock.

'That should do it.' His mouth was level with Hero's ear. She could feel his damp breath. She felt sick.

Hero knew he had boots on, no point in stamping, but she looked down. He was wearing old-fashioned breeches and thin stockings. Right! She scraped her shod heel down his barely covered shin. Webster loosed his grip. At that moment Hero elbowed him hard in the groin. Webster wailed.

'Tricks again?' Tyndall slapped her hard around the face. 'I'm not sure,' he slapped again, the other side, 'if I care,' another slap, 'what you look like when we've finished with you!'

'I think, John,' Webster could only manage a whisper, 'we should tie her hands.'

'For once, Martin, I think you're right.' Tyndall went off rummaging amongst the rags. Hero slumped down onto the floor. The leg-iron was as firm as ever. Where was Daniel? Hero thought. The yard door flapped in the wind, but the courtyard was empty.

'Got it!' Tyndall had found an old leather belt. He flicked it in the air and it made a loud crack.

This is it, Hero thought, this has to really be it. Webster was still bent double, leaning over on the table. He looked up at the sound of the belt and smiled.

'What a find, Johnny, what a find.' He pushed himself up off the table and it scraped a little along the floor, then he stumbled into a bench and knocked his wet jacket and the lantern onto the floor. It was dark again. Hero watched the thin grey plume of smoke from the pile of rags where the light had fallen. She gritted her teeth, light, light, please light!

Tyndall strode towards her on one side, cracking his belt whip, and Webster staggered along on the other. Light, please light. She saw a faint glow where the rags were.

'I can smell something, Johnny.' Webster sniffed loudly. The greasy rags stank of burning sweat.

'It's the light, you bloody fool!' Tyndall put down the belt and ran towards the smoke. Both the men grabbed old coats or blankets and flapped them at the fire. They seemed to be fanning it into life and flames erupted like tiny orange flowers opening.

Webster had already started running. He shouted for Tyndall, 'Come on, John. Come on!'

Tyndall was stamping on the fire but it had spread too far. He was coughing in the smoke. Webster opened the door to the street and shouted again. Tyndall stared at Hero through the smoke. She knew he did, she could see his face lit by the yellow fire, then he was gone too. Hero pulled herself back up to the bench. The walls of the warehouse reflected orange and red, the fire was growing.

Well now, she thought to herself, I have just escaped a fate worse than death. Only problem now, is actual death. Even if the locals down Chicksand Street smelt the smoke there would be no way they could get the key from Silver to release her.

If only she could drag herself and the table nearer the open yard door she'd have a better chance of surviving.

Her insides still ached, and the smoke was making her eyes run and the back of her throat sore. The fire was bigger now, burning the rags and the clothes for selling on and the best cotton drawers for the West End. Hero felt the smoke making her head swim. She felt the pain in her guts and the smarting in her face where Tyndall had hit her and the pricking in her eyes from the smoke. She shut her eyes. The flames felt warm on her skin, and in a moment she was sitting by the big fire in The Feathers. Ez was next to her and they were looking for the potatoes they'd put in earlier to cook. The bar was filling up and Pa would have plenty of work for both of them soon. There was someone playing the fiddle. Ned, she thought—it was his favourite tune 'The Girl I Left Behind'—and Ez was telling her the old joke about the thieving grocer and the Barbary duck when she heard Daniel shouting at her from outside.

EIGHT

Hero's throat felt incredibly sore. And the inside of her nose too, as if the skin had been rubbed away with a pumice stone. She coughed, a hard dry cough, and rubbed her eyes open. She couldn't see anything at first, her eyes were sore and watery. There was hard straw sticking in her arms and legs and the smell of goats or donkeys.

One donkey. It could have been an ass. It was staring at her with long lashed brown eyes and its mouth was full of hay. Hero struggled to get up. She was in a stable, a small wooden stable with a donkey. Or an ass, it was hard to see as it was fairly dark. There were no windows, just the light that filtered in between the wooden slats.

Her dress—It was the blue one, wasn't it? It had the same sleeves—was nearly black with dirt and smoke and her arms were red and prickled. The donkey shifted and Hero squeezed herself against the far wall. It wasn't that she was scared of donkeys, it was more that she had absolutely no idea how she'd come to be here. The last thing she could remember was the rag warehouse and Tyndall and the fire. She sniffed. Everything that didn't smell of donkey smelt of fire. She remembered the leg-iron.

She had been chained up, she was sure that had been real. Hero hitched up the ragged hem of the dress—it was the blue one, there was a hint of pattern—and there round her ankle was the leg-iron. The chain dangled in space. It looked as if it had been hacked through. Had she done it herself? Had someone got her out? Her shoes had gone and her feet were bare. She sat herself down and tried hard to remember. It was no use.

The walls of the stable were boards of wood, there were plenty of holes to see out through. Outside it looked like a field, long yellow grasses and grey stones. Gravestones, she was in a graveyard. There was a green painted railing and a street of houses beyond. It looked like the graveyard they'd buried Grandpa Reuben and Lily Juliet in. It was definitely Jewish though; the flaky pale grey stones, the Star of Davids here and there, the names, still visible, Mendonca, D'Israeli, De Symons. She pushed some of the slats further apart to see better. The sun was high in the sky, it was afternoon. How long had she been sleeping? Days, weeks?

She could do with a drink.

Outside bees hummed in and out of flowers. The air was still and even though she strained to see the houses she couldn't hear or see any people. It almost felt like the countryside.

There was a street name high on the wall, Cephas Street. She had no idea where she was. It didn't look like Whitechapel, or the West End; there was less noise and dust, it looked cleaner. The city was full of buildings going up or down, the new docks, new roads, the new streets of terraces, the old houses being knocked down by teams of men. There was more space between the buildings here, and more trees.

The donkey munched on some hay noisily. Hero smiled.

'Well, donkey.' Her voice had been rasped away by the smoke and it came out as a thin whisper. 'If someone's given you hay, then someone must have given you some water.'

Hero looked into the dark of the stable and on the floor by the door was a leather bucket. There was at least five good inches of water in the bottom. Hero picked it up and drank all of it. She could feel the cool liquid rolling down her insides, soothing the soreness and smoothing some of the raspy feeling away.

She wiped her mouth with the back of her hand, gently, as the skin was sore, then patted her wet hands all over her face, her arms and her legs. She rubbed the donkey between his long ears, something was good. Outside the sun was beginning to go down. She had to get back to the city, find the compter, find Pa. She sighed. She had no shoes, a burnt frock, and a metal anklet. Someone or other, seeing her, would be bound to turn her over to her family. For her own good, of course. But she had to try. After all, she was all Pa had. She looked up at the sky, it would be completely dark in an hour or two, not a time to be stuck in a graveyard.

She made her way around the donkey and leant against the stable door. It was locked. She should have guessed. She was still locked up, still somebody's prisoner.

The stable was so badly built there would have to be some way out. Hero was working a slat loose in the far wall when she heard someone fumbling with the lock. She had managed to break off a dagger-shaped piece of wood to use as a weapon and she picked it up quickly and crouched herself in the straw. She couldn't make out who it was. Someone small, maybe Mrs Silver. No, she was far wider than whoever this was. The shape outside dropped the keys in the mud and swore. Hero relaxed and put down her weapon.

'Daniel!' she whispered. He was sweating with the effort of carrying two large sacks.

'Hero, you're all right!' He was grinning. 'I thought you might be dead!' He took two oranges and some bread out of his coat pockets. 'Here.' He threw an orange at her. 'Did you see my note?'

Hero shook her head. She had already broken the orange apart and bitten into it and her mouth was full of juice. Daniel said he thought the donkey must have eaten it.

'I didn't get back to the warehouse till late,' Daniel said, moving the donkey over and putting his bags down. 'Was it you who started the fire?'

'I never!' She spluttered orange at him. 'Those men, it was Tyndall and his mate, they knocked a lantern over. Anyway,' she started on the bread, 'how long have I been here? And how did you get me out?'

Daniel sat down. 'I really thought you were dead last night.' He looked scared, remembering. 'Your skin was greyish, and you were limp. I pinched the skin on your cheek to make you move and it didn't redden.'

'I thought I was dead last night, too.'

'You weren't moving and the fire had caught all along the back wall. It was hot as any oven in there. I put a blanket over you and dragged you out.'

'But I was chained up! You never sawed through the iron, did you?'

'No, I bit through it with my teeth, what do you think?' Daniel rolled his eyes. 'I borrowed Ikey's father's bolt cutters.' Hero looked blank. 'Ikey from school, his dad runs the hardware supplies in Camomile Street. I knew I'd never find the key. I saw that girl, one of Father's sifting girls, Deborah.'

'Debsey.'

'Debsey. She told me you were in there. She told me they'd chained you up. That made me so sick! Last night I went home and we were having supper, and I asked Father, I said, did you chain her up, Cousin Hero? And you know what he said?'

Hero shook her head.

'He said, that side of the family does not exist. It made me so angry. I was sitting there fuming. He said you would be working at the warehouse for the forseeable future, and that the money from the sale of The Feathers would go towards my education, and Rachel's trousseau, whatever that is. Something to do with weddings, as if anyone would ever marry her if she didn't have any money! She was so smug, and Mother. Hero, they're like other people, different people. Just thinking about the money from The Feathers has made them all mad.' He was pulling at the sleeve of his jacket. 'I was wondering, when The Feathers is open again, whether you and your pa, Uncle John, might put me up? I know, I know . . . If there's a problem I could try the acrobats in Deptford, so I'll be all right.'

'Don't be soft, Dan. Of course you'll be all right with us! But you still haven't told me what happened!'

Daniel was grinning now.

'The fire was pretty high. The light was bright orange and it lit up the building, like a circus. I saw you straight off. There were tears running down my eyes with the smoke, but I dragged you out under the shoulders, like this.' He demonstrated on one of the sacks. 'I knew Father would be around any minute so I had to get you away.'

'So you're telling me you carried me all the way here!'

' 'Course not! I told Big Sam the milkman you were my sister and if I didn't hide you we'd be in trouble and a half with my father. This is Lilith, pulls the cart round Whitechapel every morning.' He patted the donkey's neck. 'And this,' he pointed outside, 'is the cemetery out by Mile End, where your mother and grandpa are. Anyhow, after I'd stuck you in here I went home.'

Daniel sucked on a piece of hay, looking out between the gaps in the stable wall. Hero ate all the oranges before she realized he was quiet.

'What happened then?'

'It was madness at home. Mother screaming that you'd brought bad luck. Father worried about the stock he'd lost. They thought you died in the fire. They're cursing you, sure you're the cause of it.' Daniel looked at her. 'I'm coming to help you now, Hero. It's the least I can do, after what . . . after what Mother and Father have done.' He sighed. 'Mother actually wrote to Barbados last November. Remember when Uncle Reuben had the chest pains?'

Hero nodded. Grandpa had been so ill he'd been in bed for a month.

'Mother thought he was for it then. She wrote to your pa's owner, previous owner, Mr Owen, of Bridgetown, is that it?'

Hero didn't know, but she didn't want to say. She had heard that Grandpa had tried to pay money for Pa. That he'd tried to make him free. She wished she'd listened . . .

'Anyway,' Dan went on, 'Mother told him where to find his property. If he wanted John da Costa back he could come and get him etcetera, etcetera.'

Hero couldn't speak. It was too much. Her aunt and uncle trying to sell Pa.

'Wait, it gets worse. Thing is, there's some problem with the law, and Mr Owen couldn't take him right away. Meantime, Mother and Father are saying The Feathers and all your property is theirs!'

'But Grandpa said! He said we'd be all right. He said! The Feathers was half Pa's anyway! They can't just take it!' Hero stood up and knocked her head on a low beam. She sat back down rubbing her scalp. Grandpa always said life was unfair, and this was proof.

'I'm not going back, Hero, I'm coming with you.'

Hero's head still hurt.

'I took five guineas off Father, and we'll go back to town and find your pa. There must be something we can do, some lawyers who'll help.'

Hero smiled. She hadn't told Daniel about Pa yet. One piece of good news.

'I know where Pa is. I heard your father talking! He's in the compter, the lock-up in the Poultry!'

'The Poultry lock-up! Not a quarter of a mile from White Kennet Street!' Daniel gathered up the bags. 'What are we waiting for?' He stood up and brushed the straw from his clothes.

'Daniel! I can't go out like this! Look at me! I look like a scarecrow that's been struck by lightning!'

Daniel pointed at one of the two sacks he'd brought.

'Your things,' he said. 'You left them at the house. I thought you might need them.'

Hero reached inside. There was her other dress, and her own shawl, and an old pair of shoes.

'Daniel! Thank you!' She ferreted about some more and felt the tight curl of papers. It was almost too dark to look at them now, but she knew her mother's picture was in there safe. Hero was smiling. Pa, we're coming, she thought. It felt as if her face would split with smiling. 'Well, go outside while I change, then!'

They left Lilith in her stable at dusk and walked away through the quiet graveyard.

'Wait a bit, Dan,' Hero whispered. It seemed right to whisper here. 'I'd like to find Grandpa and my mother.' She walked away through the rows of stones. Because of the light she had to be very close to read the names.

'Dan! Here!' There was the soft brown mound for Grandpa and the pale grey stone that marked the grave of Lily Juliet da Costa. Hero stood quietly. There was the last blackbird before dark singing his heart out from the top of a chimney pot. Hero traced the outline of her mother's name. Four words and the dates: born 20 May 1774, died 5 August 1798.

'We'd better go.' Dan started walking towards a gap in the railings. Hero said goodbye to her family and followed Dan out of the graveyard and across the big wide road that led from the City out to Essex.

'Are we just walking then?' Hero's feet were pinched in her old shoes and the road into the City stretched out ahead of them into the dark. It was wider than four regular roads and lined with stalls and shacks, most of them shut for the evening. There was a massive coaching inn, blazing with light, and factories too. Hero could smell them. A tannery or perhaps a glue factory and a sign that swung and creaked in the wind that said, 'World's Finest Horn & Bone Buttons manufactured by Hand'. Hero thought of Debsey: she'd have to get a new job now.

Hero hoped it would be one where she could keep both her thumbs.

By the time they reached the turnpike at Cambridge Heath it was pitch dark. It was scarier than walking around in town because there were fewer people about. There were dogs that you didn't hear until they were snuffling at your ankles and men with no homes to go to and too much drink inside them.

A couple of shapes moved out of the dark and fell into step behind Hero and Dan. They weren't big, and they weren't wearing shoes by the sound of their footsteps. Hero heard them shuffling along behind, Dan did too, although neither of them turned round. They followed Hero and Dan for a good fifty yards, slowly getting nearer. Hero shifted her sack to the other shoulder and quickened her pace. So did Daniel. So did the boys behind them.

Hero looked sideways at Daniel; it was just a matter of time, they all knew that. Dan was checking for boltholes, but he didn't know these streets and neither did Hero. The road was wide and the courts that disappeared away to north and south looked very dark. There were a few people around, but they wouldn't be bothered seeing a gang of kids having a punch up.

Dan was thinking they should turn around and fight, surprise them. But how to tell Hero? He reached out with his arm, as if to take her hand. Hero instinctively drew hers away. It was years since she had held anyone's hand and if Daniel Silver had any ideas like that . . .

'Gotcha!' One of them lunged at Hero and caught her by the throat. 'Give us your things and then get your shoes off! An' don't try anything, I got a knife.' The smaller boy had Hero round the neck. She struggled until she felt the cold edge of a blade.

'Hero!' Dan shouted but the end of the shout was muffled as the other boy pushed him to the ground.

Hero threw her bag to the ground. 'All right, all right, I'm doing it.' She put her hands in the air.

The boy still had the knife to her throat. He was tiny, this boy, smaller than Daniel. If only she could get the knife off him.

'Shoes, now!' the boy said, jabbing the knife across her throat.

'How can I get my shoes off when you've got me round the neck?'

The boy thought. The knife dug into Hero's skin. Grandpa always said that if someone came at you with a knife you were best off running. Hero couldn't run. She looked across at Dan. The larger boy was sitting on his back and pulling his boots off.

Slowly the boy eased off with the knife. He closed his free hand hard around her wrist then he held the knife towards her stomach. Hero saw it looked worn but sharp. She wouldn't want to risk that cutting her. She bent down and made a great deal of fuss about taking one shoe off. She stood straight again and for a split second the boy looked over to where his mate, now wearing Dan's boots, had rifled through the bag and found the five guineas.

'Gold coins, Bob!' The other boy was waving them and grinning. The boy with the knife didn't look so pleased. 'Put it away, Fletch!' He looked around in the dark. There were plenty of people who might have heard that.

Hero took her chance. She hit him hard across the face with the heel of her shoe. The boy staggered backwards, dropping the knife and screaming.

'I'm bleeding, Fletch!'

He was only a boy, younger than Dan, but his face— like Debsey's—was old. Hero got her breath back, picked up her bag and swung at him with it. He staggered away into the dark.

'Fletchy, she got me!' His nose was bleeding.

Fletch was still going through Dan's bag. When he saw what Hero had done he stood up, pocketing the five guineas. 'Gold coins!' He whispered it this time.

Dan rolled over, quick as a flash, and grabbed his bag back. 'Run, Fletch!' The other boy called for him. But Fletch wasn't going without Dan's bag. Hero hitched up her skirts ready to kick him but he jumped out of the way. Dan lost his grip, but so did the boy and the contents of the bag spilled out along the road. And the boys vanished into the dark.

'The money, they've got the money!' Dan scrabbled around for his things, spread out over the road. There was his second good shirt and some other clothes; he stuffed them all back into his bag.

'It's gone now, Dan.' Hero felt around her neck. It was still sore.

'But we've got no money.' Dan dusted himself down. Hero thought for a moment that he looked close to tears. 'And my boots! My boots!' His feet were so white they almost glowed in the dark.

'That was your fault, Hero da Costa! I wanted to surprise them, turn and attack! And what did you do? What did you think? That I would possibly want to walk along in the dark holding your far-from-lily-white hand? You are so vain sometimes, Hero! Now we've got no money, I've got no shoes! What are we going to eat? Where are we going to sleep? Have you thought of that, hmm?'

Hero looked at Daniel standing in the centre of the main London road, waving his arms around, with glowing white feet, and laughed.

'What have we got to laugh about, eh? Way I see it, nothing!'

'No,' she laughed, 'absolutely nothing except your feet. I reckon we won't need a light any more!'

Daniel stomped away and Hero followed still giggling.

She caught him up and he was still looking cross. Hero felt sorry for him.

'We'll find Pa,' Hero said. 'We'll manage.' She hoped it was true.

They walked on in silence. Hero had begun to think straight. Where were they going to sleep tonight? Would she and Daniel swan into the lock-up and force the magistrates to hand over Pa to a couple of kids? She shook the thought out of her head. She would see Pa tonight at least, and tomorrow they'd be home. He'd sort it out.

Hero looked across at Daniel, trudging towards the city like his life depended on it. They were going to make it. She could almost hear the noises of the city already; people shouting at each other behind paper-thin walls. She could taste the dust and dirt in her mouth. Then, up ahead, they saw Bishopsgate. Her feet felt sore from walking, but at least she had shoes. And she knew it wouldn't be far now. She smiled at Daniel.

'Thanks for getting me out. And coming with me.'

Daniel shrugged, but Hero could tell he was pleased.

A church bell rang for eleven as they reached the city proper. Tall buildings blocked out the starry dark-blue sky. A maze of old alleys and courts was suddenly cut off by a new road. Half built skeletons of buildings seemed to grow out of falling down ones, and inns and coffee houses still open glowed with light.

Daniel seemed to be speeding up and Hero had to scuttle after him even though she was taller. He turned a corner ahead and Hero lost sight of him for a few seconds. Then suddenly he was back.

'This is it! This is Poultry!' Then he disappeared around the corner again. Hero broke into a run. She slung the sack over her shoulder with one hand and pulled up her skirts with the other. The street looked just like any other in the city. Fine brick buildings, some smart, some shabby. Hero knew the St Anne's lock-up, a dark stone building, and wondered if this one would look the same. Daniel was ahead walking crabwise studying the brass plates on the walls. Then Hero heard him stop. She looked up and he was standing in front of a building with two small columns and a heavy wooden door. She knew that was it.

Hero threw herself at the door and began hammering at it. She stood back and they both waited. When no one came they both started banging as loud and as hard as they could.

'All right! All right!' They heard a muffled voice from beyond the door, then there was the sound of bolts being drawn back, slowly, slowly, then a small square hole opened up in the door. It had a metal grille over it and behind the grille Hero could see one large milky blue eye and part of a bulbous pock-marked nose.

It spoke again: 'All right?' it said.

Hero put her face closer to the grille.

'Da Costa,' she said. 'We're looking for Mr John da Costa. We know he's here.' Hero tried to keep her voice calm but it was hard knowing that Pa was just yards, maybe feet, away. She wondered if he could hear her voice, if he knew she was here.

The nose and the eye disappeared, leaving the gap open. Hero looked through and saw the whole of the man, carrying a candle, vanish around a dark corner. There were no other people in sight. She strained to listen for any sound, but could only hear someone singing drunkenly, far away within the heart of the building.

They waited.

It seemed like an hour before he returned.

'He's coming, Dan!'

Hero watched him shuffling towards the door holding a book that was wider than his chest. She heard the noise as he put it down on a table. He was mumbling to himself, 'Da Costa, da Costa . . . ah, here we are, John da Costa. Negro, prop. The Feathers, Soho.' He looked up at Hero. 'Are you a close relation?'

'Yes, I'm his daughter!' She thought her heart would burst. The man began to smile, and inside her head he was opening the dark door and escorting them inside already. A loud bang stopped her thought.

He had slammed the big book shut.

'He left this morning!'

For a moment there was silence. Hero thought her heart had stopped. Of course he was here. But perhaps he'd been let out?

'What! On his own, with others? How?'

'This morning. I was there, eight o'clock sharp it was, and I'm wishing for my bed now, so if you don't mind.' He reached up to close the hole.

'Wait! Wait!' Hero felt dizzy.

'I'm sorry, but I am not at liberty to divulge any more information.' And he bolted the hole shut. Hero stood still. She wasn't sure if this was good or bad news.

'We've got to get back to The Feathers, Dan, as quick as we can! We've got to get back now!' She picked up the sack and started running west, as fast as she could.

'But, Hero, you don't know where you're going!' Dan shouted after her, but she had vanished around the corner at the end of the street so Daniel gave his sore feet a quick rub and hurried after her.

NINE

Hero knew exactly where she was going. She had made straight for the massive black shadow of St Paul's, and from there she knew home was just a mile or so along the Strand, past St Clement Danes, and then right when they reached the dirty white building of St Martin's-in-the-Fields.

They passed two parish constables eating pies in the lamplight of one of the houses on the north side of the Strand, but the men took no notice of Hero striding along and Dan running after, watching carefully where he put his soft feet on the hard ground.

When they finally turned up St Martin's Lane the church clock rang one o'clock. Hero felt so happy she could cry.

'You know, Dan, I know Houndsditch isn't far, but I feel so happy, coming home. I feel like I've crossed the sea a hundred times. Dan! Dan?'

Dan was yards behind her mopping at a cut on his right foot that was weeping blood.

'I'll be happy when we can stop walking.'

It wasn't long before the two of them turned into Cambridge Circus. The Feathers was dark, that was no surprise, and the windows looked boarded up. Hero swallowed. She expected this, but a part of her imagined the pub, lights blazing, full of life, and Pa standing behind the counter. The sign was still up, three fat yellowed ostrich feathers, swinging in the night breeze, creaking softly.

Hero tried the door. It was padlocked and wouldn't move an inch. She knocked and called, not too loud, she didn't want to wake the neighbours, and it seemed eerily quiet.

'Let's try the back.' Daniel hobbled around the corner into Old Compton Street. Hero could see Sara's house and the greengrocer's and the dairy. It all looked exactly the same.

'There's a gap, in the boards!' Dan called and Hero ran quickly into the courtyard where Dan was sliding back a piece of the board in the door. Hero knew that if Pa was at home he wouldn't be making his way in through a gap in the door. She sighed.

'Hero! Come on! I don't know about you, but I've got to sleep somewhere tonight.'

He disappeared through the dark hole and Hero followed him. Inside, the hallway was dark. Floorboards creaked under their feet and Dan had to steady himself on the walls. Every noise they made seemed incredibly loud. They pushed through the large dark door into the saloon. It looked huge with no furniture, like the inside of a church or synagogue.

The counter was still there, large and curved and still shining. Hero heaved her bag up onto it and stroked it. Perhaps if she was very still, or if she shut her eyes, when she opened them the bar would be full. People would be talking all around, and laughing, and someone would be playing a fiddle. Pa would be shouting for more pots and Grandpa would be half asleep in his seat by the window.

She made a pattern in the dust and laid her head down on her sack. Suddenly, through the bag, through the solid mahogany of the bar, she could hear something. It was a sharp scuttling noise and Hero felt her stomach turn over. She stopped herself, she was imagining things, making herself hear things in the dark.

'Rats!' whispered Dan. He'd heard it too. It was real.

But it was there again, and it wasn't rats.

'It's someone coming down the stairs, Dan! Quick!'

The two of them jumped on to the counter and ducked down beneath it. Two sets of footsteps, Hero thought, voices. Hero thought of Tyndall and Webster and shut her eyes. She reached out for Dan. If she was going to die at least she'd be at home, with someone who cared for her.

They heard the door to the bar push open and Dan saw that one of them had a candle. The room filled with flickering yellow light.

'Hello? Hello!'

Hero knew that voice. She stood up, Dan with her, and there was Ez, holding a saucer with a stub of candle in it. Behind him was a tall black man. Hero recognized his face; it was the crossing sweeper from Phoenix Court.

'Ez! Oh, Ez!'

He grinned, the man grinned. Hero hugged Ez across the counter.

'This here's Simon Peter, remember?' Ez said, wiping his face. 'We've been looking after the place till you came back.'

Dan jumped out and shook Simon Peter's hand. Simon Peter clapped him so hard on his back he nearly lost his balance.

Then Ez led them through to the kitchen. There was no furniture. One chair, Grandpa's favourite, a wooden-backed seat with arms, was still there, only the back was broken. There was a table made out of a door resting on a box, and another box to sit on. Simon Peter started the fire, and Ez made some coffee. Hero saw there was a whole range of little brown paper packets on the shelf above the fire. Flour, coffee, even chocolate. Ez saw her looking.

'That's your friend Sara's old man, they've been looking out for us, giving us things. He was in here last night, telling us it ain't fair as Mr da Costa's been taken away.'

There were cups; well, one was a cup with no handle, and the other was an old beer bottle, but there was not a sign of the Stafford ware set with the blue edge that they used to have. Ez saw her studying the cup.

73

'That Mrs Silver came and packed them away in crates with straw and everything. Stripped the whole place. Those blokes, remember? That first day when you went with them?' Hero nodded. 'They came the day after and took everything else.'

Daniel nodded too. He said his parents were planning to auction the lot.

'They'll make a fair bit from the pictures your pa had, Hero, and the belts Uncle Reuben and your pa won.'

'There's followers of the fancy who'd buy that stuff an'all,' Ez added, 'even if they've been in here and drunk our ale, and said what a fine fighter Mr da Costa was. Shooken his hand and everything.' Ez spat into the fire and it sizzled.

Hero drained her coffee cup. 'We went to see Pa, this evening, but he had gone. We thought he might be here.' She was so tired now even the coffee didn't make her feel more awake. She felt tired in every part of her body, her stomach, where Tyndall had punched her, her feet from walking all that way, her heart from so much sadness. She sighed. 'He's not been here?'

Ez and Simon Peter shook their heads. 'We'd not hide him from you.'

Ez said that he thought the locksmith in Frith Street would take off the leg-iron for a few pennies, but the four of them had not one penny piece between them.

Hero shrugged. 'I suppose I better just get used to it.' She yawned, then so did everyone else.

'There's blankets upstairs, but no beds,' Ez said.

It felt strange climbing the stairs of The Feathers, this empty, ghost-ship Feathers. Stranger, turning the handle of her own bedroom. It too was stripped bare inside, the window hanging open in the wind and Old Compton Street asleep outside.

In the blue-white moonlight Hero rummaged around

inside her bag. She felt for the tight curl of papers squashed flat at the bottom. She couldn't read the writing, it was scratchy and slanted and her reading wasn't that good anyway, but she thought she'd keep them if Pa needed them. They weren't important. What was, was the thin, almost see-through sheet of vellum with the portrait of her mother, still smiling.

'I'm back now, Ma,' Hero said. She stroked Lily Juliet's cheek and jammed the picture into the side of the window frame.

Then she took the blankets Ez had given her and made a kind of nest on the floor where her bed had been, curled up in it and went to sleep. Pa was not in the lock-up, she thought, turning over and trying to get comfortable on the floor. He was not in The Feathers. Had Tyndall and Uncle Silver freed him from the compter and locked him up somewhere else? Had they put him on another boat, for the silver mines of Brazil or the cotton fields of America? There were almost too many possibilities. They might even have him chained up as she had been, fighting for money anywhere in London. Hero tried to stop the thought. If only she knew where he'd gone now, if he was all right. It took Hero a long time before she fell asleep.

When she woke, she could feel the sunlight on her bare arms and hear the noises of the street, the knife grinder and the milk woman, and the boy who sold Italian peaches that came from the glasshouses in Hackney. She lay still, listening, and staring at the familiar shape of her own bedroom ceiling.

'Hero da Costa!' It was Sara. Sara Lloyd standing in the courtyard of The Feathers under Hero's window. 'Hero!'

'Sara! I'm back, I'm home.'

Sara waved. Hero looked at her friend's clear, clean skin. Her light brown hair trying its best to go straight where Sara had forced it to curl. Her dress, a new one, or as good as. Hero imagined it flying into the West End pile at the warehouse. Sara looked like a princess compared with Hero. And she was only the grocer's daughter. Sara looked up at her friend and clapped her hand to her mouth in shock. 'You look as if you've come directly from a trip to Hades, I swear! I would kiss you, but let's clean you first. If you shake yourself down and there's not too many lice I'll take you home.'

'How many is too many? Six, thirteen, three dozen?'

Sara looked worried, she creased her forehead up thinking about it. Then Hero couldn't hold it in any longer. She looked at her friend and laughed until she was nearly sick.

Daniel had already been to the pump twice and there was a jug of water on the floor of the bedroom. Sara lent her a dress and when she had cleaned up a little, Hero went down to the kitchen where Simon Peter was boiling water for chocolate. Hero could smell it, powdered Dutch chocolate, that Sara's mother kept for special occasions. Simon Peter smiled and Hero felt guilty for ever having been afraid of him. Sara sat on the good chair and Hero on the box, Dan and Ez squatted by the fire and Simon Peter ladled out the chocolate.

Ez was incredibly happy, he smiled all the time and couldn't keep still. 'Now you're back it won't be long before Mister John's home, ain't that so?'

Hero tasted the chocolate in her mouth, it tasted bitter and sweet, grainy yet velvety smooth.

'We don't know where he is though, Ez.'

'Plan was, according to my parents,' Dan said, 'to ship your pa back to Barbados, to his owner, Mr Owen.'

'My pa has no owner.'

'No, I know that, Hero, I don't mean like that. I mean the man that owned him before. Before your pa came to London, before all this.'

Simon Peter shook his head. 'Can't do that, no, sir.

You put so much as your foot on this soil, on this groun',' Simon Peter stepped out, 'you are free as the poor wretches in the workhouse at St Peter's.' He shook gently with laughter. 'You are as free as I.' He stopped laughing, very slowly, and sipped his chocolate from the side of the saucepan. 'But I tell you,' he looked at Daniel, 'I'd sooner be free as that, free as a street sweeper with cusses from folk for "good morning", than be back in the Islands with a massa an' an overseer and no sign of my children from the day they's sold.'

Nobody spoke. Hero looked at the long, thin, ragged man and wondered where his children were. Perhaps Pa had other children somewhere too. She could have half brothers or sisters. She'd always wanted a sister but it was a difficult thought. To think of Pa having another life, a life without her or Grandpa or Lily Juliet.

She didn't know exactly how old Pa was, only that he had met Grandpa Reuben in London when he was about eighteen. Old enough for children. Now Grandpa was dead and Pa was gone, she had so many questions: Why did he go and live with Grandpa? How did he know Pa would make a fighter? Where did Pa come from? What did his home look like? Was it green and lush like the graveyard in Mile End? Hotter, it's hot in the West Indies. She tried to imagine Pa as a boy. Running around with torn breeches and no shoes.

'You know what,' Simon Peter spoke again. 'I reckon as the gentlemen to help you would be the Grandsons of Africa. They know lawyers.'

'Who?'

'I know.' Ez jumped up. 'Those gentlemen that used to meet in the back bar, last Thursday evening of the month!'

Hero still looked puzzled, but Sara was nodding and smiling. 'Yes!' she said. 'The bookshop man and the other gentleman who gave Ned music lessons. Same colour as you!'

'Yes!' Hero said at last. 'And the Abolitionist! The American!'

The American. The darkest skinned man Hero had ever seen. His skin was so deep dark brown it was almost blue. He had tiny scars on his cheek; Pa had said once, she remembered, they were on purpose, like tattoos. When he spoke his voice was deep and swinging, a kind of music. Pa said that was how all Americans spoke. The man was a fighter too, an honest fighter who'd read more books than had ever been printed. One of the best. Hero smiled. That was the man they needed. Hero wished she could remember his name.

Ez couldn't either. 'But I know where the other fellow's bookshop is!' Ez said. 'Over Piccadilly, towards St James's. I used to have to take letters for Mister John.'

'I know it too!' Hero got up, she wanted to leave right away.

'I think you have to visit the smithy first.' Sara pulled on the end of the chain that dangled from the leg-iron. 'I mean to say, that is hardly the fashion to be worn around St James's, Hero, is it?'

Sara's mother gave her a few pennies and a packet of tea for the smith. She hugged her and called her 'my chicken' and Hero nearly started crying.

The forge was in an alley near St Anne's; Hero knew the smith well, he had a son a year or two older than herself. Sara had had a passion for him last spring. But the boy wasn't there, he'd left for Belgium in the army and the smith looked grim. He was pleased to see Hero and took the leg-iron off for nothing.

'If you need any help, lass,' he said, 'shout out, eh. Your father's as good as any.'

Dan still didn't have any shoes so Hero went to Piccadilly on her own. It wasn't far and it almost felt as if she was on her way to making her life back the way it was. Town was the same, the great scar of new road that led almost from the top of The Haymarket away to the north wasn't finished, but the shops selling fancies that Debsey might only dream of were all open for business. The clothes on the fashionable girls were as pale and as clean as clouds. And a street full of bookshops and milliners and embroiderers, as if no one in the West End ever needed to eat.

Julius's was a small bookshop wedged between another larger bookshop and a ladies' milliner. Hero squeezed herself through the door and along the passage that was walled each side with books. The shop reeked of musty paper and cheap black ink that came off on your hands. William Julius was sitting in the back office. Books were everywhere, piled on the table and on the floor, wobbly looking fingers of books that Hero had to skirt round until she found enough space to turn around. William Julius did not look up. His skin was the same milky brown as the Dutch chocolate and he was so wide that Hero wondered how he had managed to get into his own shop.

'Mr Julius?'

'Hmm?' William Julius put down his pen. He was not a wealthy man, but his father had been notable in society, black and white.

'Ahh, Miss, Miss . . . '

'Da Costa.' Hero put out her ungloved hand to shake and smiled.

'Of Old Compton Street, unless I'm much mistaken.'

Hero nodded,

'Ah yes, your generous and munificent father, the prize fighter, isn't it? Hard times, hard times.' William Julius picked up his pen and scribbled something into a notebook on his desk. 'I heard the magistrates at Bow Street have locked him up and thrown away the key, on the express wishes of his own in-laws no less!' He chuckled to himself, as if describing a tale from one of his own books, rather than real lives.

Hero's eyes grew wide. 'You knew?'

'Well, it's often said: those that swim with sharks will always get eaten . . . '

'What do you mean, sir?'

'The Jews of Whitechapel! He lived with them, he took their name, I believe, and you see—snap snap!' He clapped his hands together.

Hero felt the blood rising in her face; she knew she was as much Jewish as she was black. They were her people too, and men like Julius made her feel sick. Everyone was born and died. Everyone hurt, everyone bled, whoever your God was and whatever the colour of your skin.

'I came here for help, for help from the Grandsons of Africa! Noble men, I was told, noble men.'

'You see before you a noble man.'

Hero moved suddenly and a pile of books careered onto the floor.

William Julius sighed. 'No matter, no matter.'

Hero wanted to hit him. He wasn't going to help. She watched him knit his fat fingers together across his belly. The more Hero looked the more she didn't want his help anyway.

'Grandsons of Africa, sir! You're nothing more than a drinking club for old men!' She knocked another pile of books over, on purpose this time. William Julius's face darkened.

'Young woman! If it were not for us, for our fathers . . . girls like you would not be allowed to walk the streets! We would all be bound hand and foot to some master and we would not breathe the air of . . . of . . . freedom!' His eyes were almost popping out of his head. 'I wish you to leave, now!' He stood up and began walking her out of the shop.

Hero shook his arm off and walked out by herself. 'I wish to leave myself, sir! I have come this far without your help! And if you ever set foot in The Feathers . . . '

'The Feathers, girl, no longer exists!' William Julius shouted after her.

Out in the street the milliner's girl was changing the display in the window. Hero wished she'd kept her temper longer. She could have asked for the Abolitionist's name. She looked back at the shop one last time. She could put a stone through his window, that would make her feel better. There was a display in Julius's too, above the half wooden shutters. Hero stopped. A pile of uniform green cloth-bound books stood in a better organized pile. In black letters: 'A Tale of The Trade; Being a True and Honest Account of the Full and Compleat Life of Gabriel Cuffay, Slave, Fighter, and Man of Law.'

Gabriel Cuffay, the American. That was the American's name!

She slipped back into the shop and picked up a book from the window; the pages were thin as a Bible's.

Julius's apprentice shouted at her. 'Oi, miss! Sir just threw you out!'

She scanned the frontispiece. If only her reading were better. 'I'm going, really.'

Printed by, Bound by, Year of our Lord etc, etc. Gabriel Cuffay of Portugal Street, London. Yes! She snapped the book shut and ran out of the shop as fast as she could.

TEN

Hero ran through the crowds in Mayfair, dodging the people and barrows and horses. Gabriel Cuffay, and Portugal Street only the other side of Holborn! Wait until she told Daniel! Cuffay was a tall man, as big as her father, just the man if Tyndall and Webster had Pa in the hold of some ship, or tied up in some basement. But what if Cuffay was of the same mind as Julius? She prayed not.

Once when she was younger, they'd had Passover at the Silvers', sitting around the shiny dining table and eating lamb with bitter herbs. Hero had been put next to Rachel, who had kicked her under the table during prayers and afterwards told her, 'God doesn't love you.'

Rachel had held her own naked, freckled forearm alongside Hero's. 'See—these,' she pointed at her freckles, 'kisses from God. No niggers have them. Proves it. And we're chosen, chosen specially by God. Niggers can't be Jews. You wait till judgement comes. You'll burn in Hell!' Rachel poked her finger at Hero until Hero grabbed the freckled forearm and gave her a skin burn.

That year Hero refused to go to the Silvers' for Rosh Hashanah. When Grandpa asked her why, she said, 'I'm not Jewish, Grandpa, Rachel says.'

Grandpa Reuben told her about African Jews, from Ethiopia in the east, from Morocco and Algeria in the north. 'We've probably family there still,' he rubbed his beard, 'in Fez, I think. We're Sephardi, and there probably aren't many corners of Africa a Jew hasn't seen!' He said something else too: 'Hero, whatever you want to be, you are.'

She wished he wasn't dead. None of this would have happened if Grandpa had still been alive.

By the time she reached The Feathers her eyes were watering. Inside Dan, Ez, and Simon Peter were rolling up bedding and clearing up. 'What are you doing?'

'We're making plans, Hero.' Dan was clomping about in a pair of Ned's old boots that were far too big. 'I've got to go back to the compter, someone must have seen him go. My parents didn't say anything yesterday about him going. Maybe the man from Barbados took him.' Hero went cold. She hadn't thought of that. 'I'm going with Simon Peter. You ought to stay here in case there's word.'

Hero looked at him puzzled.

'A messenger or something! If he's safe, if he's all right . . . '

'No one knows we're here, Dan.'

'They will do soon,' Simon Peter said. 'Daniel's parents will find out soon enough.'

'If they bother asking,' Dan said.

'And they will. They'll be looking for you, Dan, you know it, and someone's bound to tell them you're here,' Hero said.

'All the more reason for me to be somewhere else.' Daniel stood up. 'And I'm not scared of my parents. I'm twelve in a month, I can go where I choose, be apprenticed.'

'Or end up in the workhouse.'

'I'll be all right. They'll not come here.' Daniel didn't look at her when he said this, as if he knew it was a lie. Hero thought it was probably the second, if not the first, place they'd look. But she shook the thought away; she wanted to go and find Cuffay.

'I'm not staying here doing nothing. Listen, I've been to Julius's, I know the name of the American, it's Gabriel Cuffay!'

Dan seemed too busy to notice.

'Hero, that could be just a wild goose chase. The important thing is to find your pa before he's put on a boat.'

Ez and Simon Peter nodded.

'Everything's under control. We'll go to the compter, and Ez will go back to White Kennet Street and see what whisperings are going on there.'

'Why don't I go with him?' Hero asked.

'Don't be ragheaded! They'll see you a mile off.'

'So I should just stay here then and fetch some water?' Daniel didn't hear the sarcasm in her voice.

'If you want, but Ez has filled the jugs already, haven't you, Ez?'

Ez nodded. Hero sighed. They all left.

Hero walked into every empty room in the inn, opening windows and letting the smelly London air blow into the stale, shut up rooms. When Grandpa had died and his body was laid out, Hero knew it wasn't him, it was just the outside. Like an old jacket taken off, the real Grandpa Reuben had gone. And now The Feathers was the same. Not alive, not lived in, just a shell. From the top room she could see the Lloyds' shop, Sara standing in the doorway sweeping the dust into the gutter. She watched Sara making cow eyes at three red-coated soldiers home from fighting the French, then she looked the other way, south, and watched the jumble of carts and buggies squeeze their way down towards Charing Cross, piled high with firewood or wrapped fleeces, furniture, or feathers. The city going about its business just the same.

At the crossing where Simon Peter had worked was a small light-brown boy with straight black hair; the broom looked far too big and heavy for him. Hero thought about taking him some water when a large cart, open sided, like the one Mrs Silver had hired to move the furniture out of The Feathers, almost collided with the ripe peach boy. The ripe peach boy swore worse than a sailor and Hero laughed. She stopped laughing when she saw a small red-headed figure picking her way along the roadside, avoiding the horse and the dog turds and swishing between the knife sharpener and the song sheet seller.

Rachel Silver.

Hero pulled herself under the windowsill and crouched down on the floor. What was she doing here? Hero calmed herself down, what could Rachel Silver possibly do to her, anyway? It might not have been Rachel, it might have been anyone. She looked out again. There was no mistake, no one else walked the way Rachel did, as if she owned the street, and she was making straight for The Feathers.

Hero would go out and meet her, show she wasn't scared. Hero ran down the stairs, through the kitchen and opened the door to the yard. The afternoon sun was strong and yellow. Hero pictured Rachel rounding the corner to Old Compton Street, her hair bouncing with each step. She went back into the kitchen and picked up the stone bottle that was by the grate, felt it heavy in her hand. She imagined hitting Rachel hard across the back of the head, then tying her hands and feet and shutting her in the cellar. See how she liked it.

Rachel pushed the kitchen door open.

Hero raised the bottle.

'Dan? Daniel?' Hero heard the catch in her voice. Rachel was scared. Hero lowered the bottle and stepped out where Rachel could see her. Rachel jumped a little and put her hand to her throat, like her mother would have done.

'You! We thought you were dead!' Rachel paled.

'I'm no ghost.' Hero put the stone bottle down behind her on the box.

'Is our Daniel with you?'

Hero shrugged.

'Only Mother's having the vapours. She won't move from her bed, we've had to fetch the doctor.' Rachel paused. 'Have you done anything to him?'

'Why should I care what happens to any of you? Look what you've done, look at this place.' Rachel shifted uneasily. 'I've got no father, and just a shell of a home.

Oh, and not that for very long if your family's anything to do with it.'

'If you had behaved we would have looked after you!'

'Behaved! Behaved?'

'You attacked Mother, ran away, and burned down the warehouse. We lost a lot of money, you know!' Rachel sounded peeved.

'I'm so sorry.' Hero wanted to pick up the bottle and smash her smug face in. She stopped herself, that was what she'd expect. Hero breathed deeply.

'I did not burn your precious warehouse down.' Hero tried to speak as calmly and as measured as she could. 'I hit your mother, only after she had hit me, and I "ran away" to try and find out what had happened to Pa.'

Rachel sat down on the chair. 'Ha! Your pa! I'd have thought you'd be better off without him, brought up in a respectable household. I mean, you could pass as Spanish or It—'

Hero lunged for Rachel and pulled her out of the chair by her red curls. She pushed Rachel against the wall and drew back her fist.

Rachel squealed. 'Not my face, no!'

Hero stopped, her large brown knuckle was a breath from Rachel's freckled cheek.

'Please.'

Hero looked at her, she was terrified. What would be the point? Hero shook Rachel away and Rachel crouched in a ball on the floor whimpering. She didn't look chosen at all.

Hero felt suddenly sorry for her. She was spiteful and ignorant and she would probably remain spiteful and ignorant all her life. She would marry a rag merchant like her father, and produce a stream of rag merchant babies.

'Daniel's alive. He's well as you are, better perhaps. He has a cut on his foot—someone stole his shoes—but he's well.'

Hero walked to the other side of the room in case she

was tempted to hit her again. She lit the fire from the blackened tinder box and put a pot of water on to boil.

'Sit down.' Hero pointed at the chair. 'I'll make some chocolate, he'll be back in a while.'

Rachel sat down meekly. She was still sobbing.

Hero grew bored listening to Rachel sniffling. She looked outside, it was early afternoon and the others wouldn't be back for ages. Hero got up. She would go and see Sara, Rachel made her nervous. She imagined Mrs Silver bustling in behind her with Tyndall and being chained up again. Hero slipped a shawl around her shoulders and told Rachel she was off to fetch some firewood. Hero made straight for Sara's shop. Sara was behind the counter weighing out flour into brown paper bags.

'You'll never believe it!'

'Astound me.'

'Rachel Silver is sitting in our kitchen drinking chocolate that I made for her.'

'Are you sure you're feeling quite well, Hero?'

'I felt sorry for her.' Hero ducked under the counter and tied on an apron.

'I am truly astounded. I'd have thought you'd have blackened her eyes or broken her ribs given half the chance.'

Hero began sealing the bags for Sara. 'It wouldn't be fair. She's got no brain.'

'And you have?'

'More than her anyway.'

'Where are the others?'

'Not back from their heroic quests to find my pa. Left me stuck at home they did. Me, who knows where the Abolitionist lives.'

'You found him?'

'Well, not quite, but I know where he lives—Portugal Street.'

'By the Strand?'

'Unless there's another. Dan and Simon Peter went back to the compter and Ez went off to spy on the Silvers.'

'You should watch that they're not coming after you. I reckon you should stay with us.'

'Thanks, Sar, but I'll be fine.'

'No! The more I think about it the more I'm sure. If Rachel knows where you are it's only a matter of time before your aunt and uncle do too. That aunt of yours could come back with those men and what's Daniel going to do? Or Ez, or indeed Simon Peter. He may be a grown man but there's no muscles on him.'

Hero began to feel uncomfortable. What if she was right?

'And another thing.' Sara waved at her with the flour scoop. 'How do you know Rachel didn't tell her ma and pa where she was going? You go and get your things now, Hero, so there's not a sign that you were ever there.'

Hero felt suddenly worried. She untied the apron and ran out of the shop, across the street, and back into the kitchen at The Feathers. Rachel wasn't there. The fire was burning and the cup of chocolate lay drained on the floor. Hero pushed through into the saloon.

'Rachel?'

Hero heard movement upstairs. She's snooping, Hero thought, and legged it up the stairs three steps at a time. Hero crashed through into her bedroom as Rachel threw down Hero's bag. Rachel's face was as pink as the skinned rabbits Hero had seen in the butcher's in Frith Street.

'Hero!'

'You sneak! You nasty sneak! I have nothing and you still want it!'

'Stealing? You're accusing me of stealing from you!'

'So what are you doing then? Checking I haven't chopped your brother up into a thousand pieces and stuffed him in that bag?

Hero picked up the bag from the floor.

'It is from my father's warehouse, I recognize it. It might have been ours.'

Hero stopped listening. What did Rachel want with any of her things? She checked inside, perhaps Rachel had just put something in there, perhaps she planned to accuse Hero of theft? Hero felt around, then emptied the bag out onto the floor.

Rachel was still wittering on about property. Hero checked through her things: the jacket Daniel had given her, a shawl from home, the mourning dress she had forgotten to return. Everything seemed there. Hero looked up at Rachel, the portrait of Lily Juliet behind her on the window frame. Pa's papers! Quickly Hero looked again. They weren't there.

'You've taken something—papers. They were in here. I know you've got them.'

Rachel went deeper pink.

'Hero da Costa, I have taken nothing.'

'Liar!'

'How dare you!' Rachel was almost shaking. 'I don't have any idea what you're talking about.'

'Rachel, I have had enough of this. Of course you took them! I've also had enough of shouting and threats, it's stupid. I'm bigger than you, I'm faster than you. I'll get them back.'

Rachel bolted for the stairs and Hero ran after her.

Rachel cluttered down the first flight then her dress caught on a skewed banister and she fell and rolled all the way down to the bottom.

'Rachel!'

Hero ran after her. Rachel was face down on the floor, her arms out, her face pale. She's always pale, Hero thought, trying to reassure herself.

'Rachel! Rachel! Are you all right?'

Hero gingerly turned her over. She was breathing, her chest rose and fell, but she made no sound. There was a graze on her temple, and a cut on her white arm, only a small one, but it wept red blood in a thin trickle.

Hero tried slapping her lightly round the face.

'Wake up, wake up!' But Rachel didn't. She fetched some water in the stone bottle—'The one I was going to clout you with!'—and pulled Rachel against the wall so she was sitting. She cradled Rachel and held the water to her lips. As she did so she heard the roll of Pa's papers crackle in a fold of Rachel's dress.

Rachel groaned. Hero fed her more water. Rachel's eyes flickered open.

'Are you all right?' Hero asked.

Rachel shut her eyes and opened them again.

'My shoulder . . . ' She shifted herself more upright and flinched with pain.

'Drink this.' Hero put the stone bottle into Rachel's right hand and closed her fingers around it. Then Hero took the roll of papers from the pouch at Rachel's waist. Rachel didn't move.

'You can't win,' Rachel said closing her eyes. 'My parents will come. They'll take you back. They'll find your pa, you're only making things worse.'

'How can things be worse for me?'

Rachel looked at her. 'The auction, remember? Soon enough you won't even have anywhere to sleep.'

Hero stood up slowly, she had to fight the impulse to batter Rachel's face in with the stone bottle. Then no one, not even the idiot's son, would look at her. She held the papers tight in her hand. She thought of Pa and Grandpa; you couldn't hit someone when they were lying down, even if you'd be doing the world a favour.

'I'm going now. Daniel will come soon. He'll look after you.'

Then Hero ran out of The Feathers and into the street, where it was just beginning to get dark.

ELEVEN

Hero ran smack into Ez. He was out of breath and wet with sweat.

'Ez! What happened?'

'Go, Hero, now! The Silvers are coming, Ma Silver any rate, with her heavies. Someone's seen you, told 'em you were here. They got spies or as good as! There was so much shouting and yelling from that house you could hear their doings from Ludgate.' Ez was smiling, pleased with himself for finding so much out. 'What's wrong?'

'I've got to go anyway, Ez.' She was almost weeping, she didn't know why.

'All right, all right. I'll clear out our stuff from The Feathers, we can hole up somewhere. I'll wait for your Dan and Simon Peter at the Lloyds'.'

'Rachel Silver's in there, she's hurt.'

'What! Dan's sister? What did you do to her?'

'I never laid one finger on her, Ez. She fell, down the stairs, went into a faint . . . I can't stay in there with her or I swear I will clout her all the way to heaven.'

'You better go. Me an' Dan'll sort it out, or get beaten up trying.'

'Any sign of my pa?'

Ez shook his head. 'Only good thing is as those Silvers haven't either.' Ez smiled. 'And mad as hell they are about it too!'

Hero ran across to Sara's, the lamps inside the shop had been lit and she could see Sara and Ned laughing with a customer.

'Sar!' She pushed through the door making the shop bell ring wildly. The laughing stopped.

'Hero, what on earth has happened?' Sara lifted the

hinged counter and led her friend through to the back of the shop. 'You're pale as a sheet!'

'I never touched her, Sar! She was after these, she had taken them out of my room.' Hero handed the pile of papers to Sara.

'Shush, shush yourself.' Sara fetched a drink for Hero and sat her down in the store room at the back of the shop while she explained. Sara unrolled the stiff, crackly papers. 'What are they?'

'I don't know, they were Pa's or Grandpa Reuben's. I can't read them, the writing . . . But they must be important, worth something . . . '

Sara held them up to the lamplight. 'My reading's worse than yours. Where's Rachel now?'

'Still at The Feathers, she's hurt her shoulder. Ez came back though, he says the Silvers don't know where Pa is either, and they're out to find him.'

'Well, you can stay here, we'll mind you.'

Hero shook her head. 'No, Sar, thanks all the same. Pa seems to have vanished off the face of the earth and I've got to find him before those Silvers do. Listen, keep these papers safe, they must be precious. Ask Daniel to read them, he can read anything, even Hebrew.'

Sara hugged her tight. 'Where are you going, Hero?'

'I'll go and see that Cuffay, perhaps he knows something.'

'Are you sure?'

Hero nodded. 'I have to keep looking. I can't just do nothing.'

'But where'll you sleep? There's all sorts out there on the streets of a night.'

'I tell you, Sar,' Hero said, 'I can sleep anywhere without an iron ring round my ankle.'

Sara gave her a few oatcakes in a shop bag and let her out the back way in case anyone was watching. It occurred to Hero that her life now was nothing less than the melodramatic lives of girls or young men that the street singers sang songs about. Men who would be hanged three times and never die, girls who would go to sea in breeches, or kill their wicked uncles. Perhaps, Hero imagined, there would be a song about Hero da Costa, the pugilist's daughter. Hero stopped herself. Very often the songs ended with the heroine with a knife in her heart or the young hero on a boat bound for Van Diemen's Land. Hero wanted a happy ending, but that was hard to imagine. Even if she found Pa, they would need a hoard of money to restore The Feathers. That's if she found him before the Silvers sold it. Surely you couldn't sell something that wasn't yours in the first place. Life was getting more and more complicated.

Hero crept along the mews behind the shops of Old Compton Street. Piles of waste and rubbish made the stink worse than that in the wider, cleaner, street. When she reached Cambridge Circus she scanned the evening crowds just in case. She strained to catch sight of any Silvers, either the small, wide mistress recovered from the vapours and out for revenge, or the pinched, darker master; not a sign. She looked, too, for Daniel, snaking his way through the stalls, or the familiar dark, stretched figure of Simon Peter. There was no one.

She ran across the open space and down into Earlham Street, towards Seven Dials, the heart of the parish of St Giles. It was the quickest, if not the safest, route, Pa told her, and if you cross St Giles, cross it in the daylight. They'll all rob you blind soon as look at you, he always said, and Grandpa Reuben would nod in agreement. But Hero thought to herself that it couldn't be any worse than the docks in the dead of night, and it was the quickest way to Portugal Street.

The streets were dark and narrow, the old buildings seemed to reach up and shadow the streets like huge trees, almost meeting at the top to block out the sky. They seemed crammed with people, the windows were all flung open and blankets and rags flapped out to air or to dry, Hero wasn't sure which. She quickened her step and watched her feet to avoid turds and the thin treacly river of filth that snaked down the centre of the narrow alley. Hero had heard that in the inns that marked the corners of streets they had fights, fights with no rules, that Grandpa would sometimes go and watch. Grandpa said he was still looking for a fighter better than Pa, someone he could train up. But Pa said he just enjoyed the sight of one man knocking the other's brains out.

Hero didn't really like boxing. She knew that for Pa it was a means to an end, a way out of one life and into another. Grandpa Reuben, though, loved a good fight.

In a doorway to one of the tall, narrow buildings a girl met Hero's gaze; she had a baby on her hip and a toddler clutching her dress. She was almost a mirror to Hero, same hair, same eyes, same brown, brown skin. If Pa was hiding anywhere in London, these streets, these buildings stuffed to the gills with the poor of London would be just the place. There were Negroes of all shades from Africa, America, every island of the West Indies, East Indians, and Lascars who had given up waiting for a boat home; Irish and all the poor whites who couldn't get work in service or digging up the roads for canals or building new houses for the gentry, all squashed together in the one parish.

But for the grace of God, your Grandpa Reuben, and my fists, Pa often said, St Giles is where we'd be. And where we may be yet, Hero thought to herself.

Hero tried to hold her breath until the roads had widened out and she reached the market place at Covent Garden, where the rich were filling up the theatres and their carriages and cabs crammed the streets. She passed in front of the grand Theatre Royal which was an impressive building even by London standards, with two great blazing gas lanterns the size of cauldrons making hissing noises like twin snakes, then it was only steps down at last to where the traffic threaded north up to Holborn. Hero stopped a while scanning the crowds for familiar faces, hoping that the Silvers or Tyndall wouldn't grab her the moment she stepped out into the wide main road. She could just about see Portugal Street on the other side.

The sky was navy blue and the stars were out and she hoped that wherever Pa was he was all right. Perhaps Daniel and Simon Peter had found him already. Or perhaps the Silvers had got to him first. Perhaps it was all too late and Mr Owen the owner had reached out from across the sea and grabbed Pa himself, tired of waiting for the Silvers to deliver the goods. Despairing rubbish, Hero said to herself, she could waste all night with perhapses and be none the wiser. Cuffay could turn her away like Julius, or welcome her in and tell her that he had seen Pa in the compter for himself. She would never know until she asked. Hero crossed the wide main road and turned into the first small side street. She would ask directly, at the first inn or shop she found open, which house was Mr Cuffay's.

She didn't have to. Hero looked up at the well proportioned brick town houses around her; they all had three or four storeys, and neat white steps up to freshly painted black doors. Some had brass plaques next to round bell pulls. She ran up the steps of the first house, number two, and peered at the writing. She could just about read the words as the letters were nice and clear, large plain capitals, not fancy copperplate or scratchy handwriting. It said: Gabriel Cuffay, 2 Portugal Street. Hero rang the bell.

She waited on the step for an eternity. A mother hurried past with twin babies, one tied on the front, one on the back, both bawling. A man with a barrow of logs for sale trundled past. Hero looked up at the house. There were lamps lit, someone was at home. She rang again. Somewhere deep inside the house she could hear footsteps, running, skipping down the stairs, then slowing to a walk across the hall. Hero heard the bolts draw back and straightened herself, ready to speak. The door opened and a dark brown face in a bright white servant's cap opened the door wider than a crack, but not much more. The girl's eyes were sharp as stars as she looked Hero up and down.

'Yes?' She spoke with an American accent.

'Please, I'm looking for Mr Cuffay, is he at home?'

'Mr Cuffay isn't seeing visitors.' The girl made to shut the door.

'Please! Please wait! It's important, very important. It's about Mr da Costa, the publican! The fighter.'

The girl moved slowly. 'I said, Mr Cuffay ain't seeing visitors—and even if he was, which he's not—he ain't at home.'

'Do you know when he's coming back? May I not wait for him?'

The girl sighed. 'Mr Cuffay left me saying as I wasn't to let anyone in on any account. What's that name you mentioned again?'

'Da Costa, John da Costa!'

The girl looked up and down the street. Was she looking to see if Hero had anyone else with her, or if she was being followed? Hero thought for a moment the girl was about to open the door wide. There was, after all, a flicker of recognition when she'd heard Pa's name.

'I'm his daughter!'

The girl looked at Hero closely. She didn't look as if she believed it.

'Well, Mr Cuffay said as how I shouldn't let no one in and I ain't going to start crossing him now.' And she slammed the door.

Hero shouted, she pressed herself against the closed door. 'But when's Mr Cuffay coming back? You could tell me that!'

Hero put her ear to the door and heard the girl's footsteps shuffling away down the hall. She stood against the shiny black door and pulled her shawl around her. She would swear on Pa's life that the girl knew Pa's name. She looked up at the windows and realized that the shutters were being closed, as much against her, she suspected, as the night. There were steps down to the area and a door, which Hero thought must lead into the kitchen. She padded quietly down but the door was locked. It began to rain, a very soft fine rain, but since Hero was not dressed for the weather she huddled in the shelter of the area door. Perhaps there was another way in. Daniel would be scrabbling over the rooftops or scaling yard walls. But what if she got in and it was a waste of time, they knew nothing of Pa and they called the parish constables? That was stupid, Hero thought, after all she had absolutely nothing to lose. She waited until the rain eased off and cut around to the back of the terrace.

There was a narrow passage between the houses of Portugal Street and the next street along. High brick walls, some with wooden doors, rose up on either side. Hero found the back door to the Cuffay house but that was locked too—she turned the handle furiously, leant against it with all her weight, but nothing happened. A dog started barking in one of the yards, somewhere a child was crying, and, further along again, a girl was singing 'Green Gravel'. Perhaps she could climb over instead.

Hero wound her shawl around herself and tied the ends across her chest then looked for something to stand on. She found a wooden bucket and up-ended it against the back door. Hero hauled herself up. For once she was glad she was tall; if she had been Sara, she would not have been able to see anything, even standing on a bucket. But Hero could see into the back scullery where the American girl was polishing a large metal bowl. She looked up a storey, the window was dark, up another and she could see into a bedroom. There was no one moving around, but she could see that Mr Cuffay was reasonably well off; there were paintings and the curtains were heavy and expensive looking. There was one more room unlit, right at the top of the house, a tiny dormer window. The angle was too high, so Hero couldn't see into it, but she thought it must be the girl's attic room.

As Hero was watching she heard the bell ring at the front of the house and watched as the servant put down her work and scurried off to answer it.

This was her chance. Hero put her forearms along the top of the door and heaved herself up. Then she swung one leg over the top of the door and was sitting on top of it. She paused. If that bell was Cuffay returned, she could go around to the front of the house and ask to see him, like a regular visitor. But the longer she sat on the top of the door the more likely it was a neighbour would spot her.

She jumped down quickly into the yard, as she heard the front door slam shut. She came crashing down—somehow the yard was lower than the alley outside—and fell hard on her ankle. She heard her dress tear too, a long thin ripping sound as it split from the waist, which was high, in the fashion, to the hem. She was tying the ends together as she heard voices, three, laughing and walking through the house.

Hero looked around. The yard was bare: a stack of firewood and an empty barrel. She wouldn't fit inside it. She ducked under the window and hoped no one would see her.

The voices receded. The maid came back into the scullery. Hero heard a voice call out—Cuffay's—'Fetch us some wine, Liza', and a door shut upstairs. Liza busied herself with glasses and as soon as she'd gone, Hero pushed through the back door, shut but not locked, and along the passage.

Hero heard Cuffay's deep American voice again. 'Thank you, Liza.'

And the maid shut the door, then she knocked again. 'Beg pardon, Mr Cuffay, but a girl came by the house, not long ago, sir. She said she was looking for Mr da Costa. I sent her away, as you said, Mr Cuffay, we weren't to have visitors.'

Hero listened in the dark at the foot of the basement stairs. Cuffay spoke again, 'What was she like, this girl?'

'Oh, sir, if I hadn't known any better I'd have said as how she were almost a giant!'

There was a spluttering noise and another voice: 'That sounds like my daughter and you turned her away!'

Hero felt the dissolving feeling in her legs. She felt the tips of her fingers and the joints of her knees go fluid. 'Pa!' Her voice came out like a little squeak. It was! It was! She forced herself to move, how could she keel over now, never seeing him, the idea was too awful.

In her mind she was running up the stairs, barging into the room, and holding on to him so tight. In this reality, right now, she could only drag one foot in front of the other up the stairs. It felt as if she had a hundred shackles around each ankle.

She could have imagined it. Minds play tricks. She could push the door open and it could be some mirage, some dream.

'Pa!' She managed it louder and then Liza dropped her metal tray, breaking the air with an enormous clanging.

'Lord preserve us!'

'Pa!'

'Hero!'

It was Pa. He picked her up on the stairs and brought her into the well lit parlour.

'That's the girl! That's the one!' Liza's mouth was hanging open.

Pa was grinning so as his face would split apart.

'Fetch her some water, Liza! Please!' Gabriel Cuffay put down his wine glass. 'Well, well.' He was smiling too.

Hero knew it was real, the sound of Pa's voice, the familiar smell of his skin.

'Pa! You're here! I've been looking everywhere!'

TWELVE

That night Hero slept in a bed with fresh cotton sheets. They were so white and dazzling that in the morning it took her a long time before she could fully open her eyes. She stretched and felt her face ache from smiling.

There was a knock at the door and Liza brought in a tray with warm rolls and honey and a cup of coffee. Hero kept thinking she was dreaming but she touched the side of the coffee cup and it was hot. She put her finger in the honey pot and licked it, it tasted sweet. Liza was opening the curtains and the sun was already high up in the sky.

'Excuse me, but how long have I slept?'

'Oh, it's near enough noon, but Mr Cuffay said not to wake you.'

'Is my father still here?'

'Well, he's not gone out this morning, miss.' Liza was smiling.

Hero spread one of the rolls with honey and bit into it.

It was all real. Pa was sitting in the parlour in a battered leather armchair when she went downstairs. He was talking to Cuffay who was leaning against the fireplace, smoking a long-handled pipe. Hero paused outside the room, just watching and listening.

Last night, Mr Cuffay explained how he had been advising Pa, working to get him out of the compter, prevent Pa's kidnapping, and establish his safety. These were difficult times, Cuffay said, to be a Negro. The law was unclear. He had tried to explain it; that slavery existed in the Empire, but slaves could no longer be traded. Hero had nodded but she really didn't see the difference. That Pa couldn't be forced to return to Barbados, but if he was kidnapped, well . . .

Hero felt ashamed; in her small world she had felt that she was protected, apart from whatever trials and tribulations Negroes faced every day.

She was always just special, different, darker skinned obviously, but with hair that curled into fashionable Greek-style ringlets by itself, and if occasionally people shouted at her in the street, she knew it was their ignorance, and it never touched her.

Hero did not think of herself as a mulatto, but as the daughter of John and Lily Juliet da Costa. Until Pa had been arrested and she'd been sent to the Silvers', Hero hardly thought about her colour. Lately it seemed that her skin colour had mapped her fate. Cuffay was reading a letter to Pa from a firm of lawyers and Pa was nodding and smiling. Hero still hovered in the doorway, scared that she might break the spell if she moved.

'Hero!' Pa had seen her. 'Great news! Cuffay here has word from his lawyers. The Silvers have no right to detain me and Mr Owen from Barbados has no claim on me either!'

Hero wasn't so sure. She sat on the arm of Pa's chair. 'But what if they kidnap you? They've heavies, a man called Tyndall and another; big men, I think they work for Owen, on his ships.'

Pa nodded. 'The Silvers wrote to Owen last winter, when Grandpa was ill, remember? Those men will be on their way back to the West Indies without me very soon. I don't think we should worry too much about them.'

'Is this true?' Hero looked up at Cuffay. He nodded. 'All true.'

Hero felt as if a stone had been lifted from her heart.

'So why don't we go back to The Feathers; get all the furniture back from the Silvers? Why don't we just go home, Pa?'

'That's where we still have a problem.' Pa sighed. Cuffay bent down and cleaned out his pipe into the fire.

'Your father's right. See, your aunt and uncle claim The Feathers is theirs.'

'But how can that be, Pa?'

'They want to prove that we're not Grandpa Reuben's family, that he didn't recognize us, and he would never have left The Feathers to me.'

Hero thought for a while. That was ridiculous. Anyone who knew Grandpa, any of the punters who ever drank in The Feathers, how could any judge be persuaded that Grandpa wasn't her grandpa?

'That won't work, will it, Pa?'

Pa shifted in the armchair. 'To a judge, Hero, a white man leaving his worldly goods to a Negro, even a Negro who married his daughter . . . '

'Especially a Negro that married his daughter!' Cuffay added.

'To a judge, a white judge, that looks all wrong. The Silvers are trying to prove your grandpa never felt for me—or you.'

'But Grandpa used to say you were like his own son, I heard him!'

'That's not proof, darling.'

'Wait, wait, I know where there's proof! I know! On the sign above the door, in gilt paint: Prop. Reuben da Costa and Son—and Son!'

Pa put his hand on Hero's to calm her. 'Hero, girl, calm down. That's not the proof that will fix things for us.'

Cuffay shook his head. 'But didn't you say, John, the old man made a will?'

'Grandpa Reuben was sharp as a knife. He knew something like this might happen, so you know what he did? He swore with witnesses, Mr Lloyd and the rabbi from the synagogue at Bevis Marks, that everything he had was ours, which was no more than the truth anyway.'

'So why don't you show the judge?'

'Didn't you say that the Silvers cleaned every last stick of furniture out of The Feathers?'

Hero nodded.

'Well, they'll have the papers right in their hands, and if I'm not much mistaken, they'll all have been burned to nothing and the smoke will be halfway up to heaven by now.'

'No, Pa.' Hero was getting excited. She pulled Pa up. 'No, Pa, I know exactly where those papers are.' She crossed her fingers. 'Were they rolled up with that picture of Ma?'

Pa nodded.

'Then they're safe! Safe at the Lloyds' dairy and provisions shop with Sara!'

Pa kissed her. 'What are we waiting for, Gabe! Send Liza out for a brougham, no, I can still make it across town faster than some fly-blown, cow-hocked hired nag. Let's run. Hero, come on!'

'My dress!' It was still torn up the back.

'Never mind about the dress. Cuffay, you've a cloak for the girl? We'll run!'

Pa pulled Hero along with him out of the front door and down the white steps into Portugal Street. Hero held on to his hand tight, taking two steps for every one of his. Her cloak was hot and felt as heavy as lead. They reached Covent Garden market, which was full and busy. Porters with towers of baskets on their heads, women with sacks of onions and carrots, the cobbles slippery with old cabbage leaves. Pa wove easily between the stalls and the horses and people, never once looking back. Hero felt every bone in her hand pulled apart as she struggled to keep up and then, through the crush of the crowd, she realized she'd let go of him. She stopped running and looked around. She couldn't see him at all; a curtain of people had shut off the streets, the roads beyond the market, and all she could see or hear was a sea of white faces and the roar of the street sellers.

'First carrots! Spring greens! Spring greens!'

'New potatoes, first this year! Small as pearls and just as pricey!'

'Pa!'

Hero felt lost in the sea of people, her voice completely drowned out. Her heart sped up until she thought it would burst in her chest. She couldn't see him. Usually, being tall, she could see over and above crowds, but there were so many people here. She hoisted herself up on a pillar scanning the market and just caught sight of Pa swinging around the corner into King Street.

'Pa!'

He hadn't noticed she was gone. Hero jumped down and raced after him, knocking two baskets of cabbages over and hearing the curses of the market porter behind her when she didn't stop.

'Pa! Wait! Pa!'

Pa swung round.

'Hero! I thought you were just behind me!'

Hero was so out of breath she leant against the wall, breathing heavily. 'I can't keep up with you, Pa.'

Pa smiled and hugged her. 'Come on then, Hero, just like old times, eh?'

And he bent down so that Hero could climb up on his back. Hero clambered up and clamped her hands tight together around his neck, and when Pa straightened up Hero felt taller than anyone in the world. Pa set off again, Hero's brown legs dangling loose like extra limbs, so that from behind the two of them looked like the eight-legged spiderman Pa used to tell her stories about when she was little. When they reached Cambridge Circus Pa set her down.

'There it is,' Pa said.

Hero could tell he was sad looking at the building, all boarded up and with the big wooden doors nailed shut.

As they got closer Hero could see the boarded windows had small printed posters glued up all over them, like the handbills advertising fights that were left in The Feathers sometimes. The letters were large and black and evenly printed and Hero realized they were nothing to do with championship battles or fairs newly arrived in town. AUCTION, they all read, a hundred times over, like a hundred voices shouting the word inside her head. BY ORDERS OF THE RIGHTFUL OWNERS, THE FEATHERS PUBLIC HOUSE, 2, OLD COMPTON STREET IN THE PARISH OF ST ANNE'S. Hero felt Pa's hand grip hers tighter. ON THE THIRD OF MAY 1810, AT THE HOLBORN TAVERN. NOON.

'They've brought the auction forward,' Pa whispered.

It was only two days away now, Hero thought. 'Don't worry, Pa, we'll be all right.' Hero squeezed his hand. Pa didn't say anything and Hero hoped she was right. 'I think we ought to go to the Lloyds' first.'

They almost tiptoed around the inn. Hero listened hard for Rachel, or any sign of movement, but there was none. They would be wondering where she had got to, Ez and Daniel. She hoped they were at least as half as happy as she was now.

Mr Lloyd clapped Pa on the back. 'John, John!' He was grinning broadly. 'I don't know when I was so glad to see a man!'

Mrs Lloyd was wiping the corners of her eyes, and sending Ned to fetch a side of lamb from the butcher in Frith Street. 'And tell him it's for John da Costa! Tell him John's home!'

Hero found Sara cleaning in the shop.

'Where's Dan and Ez and the others?'

'Where have you been, more likely, girl! They were waiting for you till they couldn't wait any longer!'

'What do you mean?'

'Old Ma Silver came not an hour after you had gone. Boxed Ez round the ears, accused first him and then you of attacking her Rachel. You never touched her did you, Hero?'

'I swear to God!'

'Well, she's got the knives out for you good and proper! Claims you ought to be dead!' Sara smiled. 'Said you'd corrupted her son and mauled her daughter.'

'Me corrupted Dan! That's rich!'

The shop bell tinkled and two women came in for salt and sugar. Hero helped bag up their goods and waited until they'd gone.

'What happened to Dan anyway? Did he have to go back with his mother?'

'No!' Sara shook her head. 'I hid him out the back in our Netty's sty. He smelt like the night-soil man's cart when I got him out!'

'You never put him in with the pig!'

'It was that or back to Whitechapel with his mother! He was in that sty covered in muck before I turned round!'

'Where is he now? Where's Ez and Simon Peter? Back at The Feathers? Only it looked so sad and quiet just now.'

'All of them's hiding out in the Seven Dials with Simon Peter. As soon as Ned's back from the butcher I'll take you.'

Pa spent the morning in the back of the shop with Mr Lloyd. Sara fetched the roll of papers Hero had left with her from where she'd hidden them at the bottom of her chest of drawers and went back to help her mother in the shop.

It took Cuffay half an hour to reach Soho. 'I walk slowly, man,' he said clapping Pa on the back. 'Helps me think.'

He sat himself down at the parlour table and studied each of the curled up sheets of paper. He peered at one particular piece so hard Hero thought the words would all fade away with being stared at. Pa and Mr Lloyd sat quiet, waiting, supping small cups of coffee.

'What do you reckon, Gabriel? Are we safe, will the judge see us within the week?'

Cuffay was frowning. He stroked his chin thoughtfully. 'They'll not listen to me, John. We'll need a white lawyer and a good one at that. One with heart enough to take this on.' He looked up from the roll of papers. 'Have you money left, John?'

'Not a penny, Gabe, not one penny.' Pa sighed.

Gabriel Cuffay bent over the papers again and Mr Lloyd poured more coffee.

'I don't see it, though.' Mr Lloyd put down the coffee pot. 'Will the judge not listen to you? The way I see it it's plain and simple: John's in-laws, not taking to his complexion, arranged to have him out of the way and flog all his assets.'

Gabriel Cuffay smiled and shook his head. 'Law is not that simple. If we are up against a magistrate who believes that Negroes are born to be the servant of the white man we can never win.'

Mr Lloyd slammed the coffee pot down on the table and some of the coffee jumped out. 'So what can you do elseways? Give in because you've not enough cash? If what you're saying is true the judge won't take any notice of a lawyer if he's black or white, if he's defending a Negro.'

Cuffay nodded.

'Land of the free!' Mr Lloyd said angrily.

'Pa, there has to be something we can do!'

'I'll find out who's on the bench, John. As far as I can see our one hope is that our magistrate is a follower of the fancy!'

Hero slipped away and found Sara leaning on a broom outside the shop watching the draper's errand boy make his way towards Charing Cross.

'Sar! Sar!'

'Hmm?' Sara watched him go and began sweeping again.

'I'm off to find the others, are you coming?'

'I can't. Mother says I've to mind the shop. I'll tell you where they are though: Dyott Street, St Giles, up by the Three Bells.'

Dyott Street was one of the oldest, darkest streets in St Giles. The buildings were crumbling and the smell was so heavy you could taste it in your mouth and even through your nose. Hero held her dress up out of the dirt and looked at the walls of buildings either side. She thought that sleeping in the hut in the graveyard would be a thousand times sweeter than living here. She didn't know who to ask; the people in the street eyed her as if she was dangerous. The women pulled their shawls around their faces and the men leered. A small child threw a stone that sped past her face. Hero almost turned to go, when up above she heard the squeal of a window being pushed open. A small, familiar head popped out and Hero was relieved.

'Ez!'

He motioned her to come up and Hero ran towards the open doorway under the window. Inside the building was worse than outside. Hero drew her hand back from the banister: where it was still fixed it was black and sticky with dirt. At the top of the first landing was a pile of vomit, she could smell it even in the gloom. The only light came from a broken skylight in the ceiling.

A door a flight up opened and Hero could see Ez waiting. 'Quick, Hero! Up here!'

The tiny room was filled with a mattress, an old lumpy straw mattress, and Simon Peter, eyes shut, was lying on it. Hero thought at first his forehead was shiny with sweat but as she got closer she saw it was sticky blood.

'Ez, what happened?' Hero whispered. Simon Peter didn't move.

'Silvers.' Ez looked scared too, he had a large purple-yellow bruise on his upper arm. 'They came for Daniel this morning. Kicking and screaming he was, but his ma had brought two heavies.'

'I know, one had no teeth.'

'Right. Anyhow, they done it for Simon Peter, laid in to him like nothing I've seen.'

'Did you get a doctor?' Hero bent over Simon Peter; she could just make out the rise and fall of his chest.

'Where would I get a quack?'

'Ez, listen, I found Pa, he's back at the Lloyds'. Go there at once and tell him what's happened, he'll know a doctor. I'm going after Dan.'

'But what about Simon Peter?'

'He doesn't know we're here, he won't know we've gone. But be quick!' Hero watched while Ez ran towards Old Compton Street then turned east and made for the City.

THIRTEEN

It was a longer walk than Hero had remembered. As she passed St Paul's she realized she had no idea what to do when she reached White Kennet Street. Knock on the door, ask if Daniel was well? A few days ago the Silvers had her chained and bound as a near enough slave. A legal slave, an indentured labourer signed up to work for nothing for the next nine years. What if they shackled her up again, forced her to sign the papers this time?

She was daft. Ez should have come to the Silvers' and she should have gone for Pa and the doctor. But Dan had always stood by her. If he hadn't dragged her out of that warehouse she'd be dead by now. It was the least she could do.

The baker's on the corner was closed for the afternoon as she turned the corner into the street. Hero could see the Silvers' house, dark and tall and from the outside ordinary and quiet. There was at least another five hours until it began to get dark. She couldn't climb up the face of the house until then, but Hero wasn't sure she could wait that long. She crossed in front of the house walking quickly in case she was seen straining to hear anything from inside. Trying to look without turning her head, she only caught a flash of the black front door and the edge of the front room curtains. She walked back and stopped by the baker's, catching her breath and thinking hard and looking at the house sideways on.

As Hero looked at the house she thought what she wanted was for them to have their cosy, well-off lives disintegrate, dissolve away as hers had. She wanted Rachel to think what life might be like without new frocks, or Mrs Silver to take coffee with her friends wearing a leg-iron. They had it so easy and they didn't know it. Pa would have told her not to waste room in her heart with bitterness. His would have burst by now, he always said. Hero didn't feel at all noble.

A man with a penny whistle crossed into the street and began to play. A few of the children who were fetching water from the pump at the far end of the street went over to listen. Hero half expected to see Rachel come down the steps with Sam on her hip. She didn't.

Hero passed the Silvers' house again, closer this time, tipping the black painted railings that fenced off the area with her fingers. Then the railings stopped, her heart jumped; it was the top of the area steps down to the kitchen and the coal cellar under the front steps. Without missing a beat Hero ducked down the steps and stopped in front of the scullery door.

Her heart was hammering against her ribs. She was sure Mrs Isaacs, moving around on the other side of the door, could hear her. Hero's chest felt so tight she could hardly breathe. There were more footsteps—someone else coming down into the kitchen—and voices, Rachel's familiar whine, Mrs Isaacs's calm and vapid, and the other, that had to be Dan's. They were arguing over Sam. It was hard to hear, Hero could only make out the edges of words and the ends or beginnings of sentences where the voices were higher or louder.

In the end there was a loud crash, a pan dropped on the stone floor, and Rachel's small clacky steps retreated into the house. Hero crouched along under the window and peeped through. Mrs Isaacs, back to the window, was picking up the pan and setting it back onto the table. She was shaking her head and muttering about a pudding that wouldn't set. Daniel was slumped in a chair at the table with his head in his hands. He looked cleaner than the last time Hero had seen him and he had two battered books in a bundle just back from school. It was easier to hear through the window.

'Now, now, Master Daniel, if you've given your word, then there's the end of it,' said Mrs Isaacs, cracking two eggs into a large bowl and whisking at them with a fork.

Daniel said nothing, he sighed and looked past Mrs Isaacs out into the area. Hero waved and Daniel almost fell off his chair.

'Well, I'll get off then, Mrs I,' he said, brighter, and ran out of the kitchen.

Hero ducked back under the stairs and listened as she heard the front door slam and Daniel jump down into the street. He swung around the railings at the entrance to the area and whispered.

'Hero?'

Hero smiled up at him from her hiding place.

'Here!'

'Ssh!' He looked around to check no one was watching. 'You can't stay here, they'll see you!'

'I've come to take you back, Dan. Pa's home, well, not home, home yet, but at the Lloyds'! He's not going to end up in Barbados!'

Daniel jumped down the steps into the area and stood next to her. 'I can't come with you, Hero.' Dan kept his eyes on the ground.

'Why ever not? You said you couldn't live with them after what they'd done.' Hero threw a tiny pebble against the area wall.

'I've promised.'

'Promised what?'

'I made them promise, too! I made them promise to call off the auction and let you and your pa have The Feathers if I go to school and start work for Father after I'm twelve. Mother said they'd forfeit all their rights, she gave me her word, Hero.'

'But the auction's going ahead, day after tomorrow, they've not called it off at all!'

Daniel didn't say anything.

'It's the truth, Dan, I swear! Pa said this morning, we can't even pay for a lawyer to call it off, to sort it out!'

Daniel kicked at the dirt at the bottom of the area. Hero had never seen him look so angry, even his eyes looked darker than usual. 'This is the truth you're telling me now, isn't it?' Hero nodded.

Hero heard the front door above their heads slam hard and she pulled Dan into the shadow of the front steps. She put her finger to her mouth.

'Daniel, I know you're there!' It was Rachel. 'Mother says you're to help me mind Samuel this afternoon, so don't go running off to Ikey's!'

Hero could see Rachel's pale freckled arm tipping the railing just as she had done earlier as she looked down the road for her brother. 'You can't be far, Dan. Come out!' Rachel peered down into the area and Hero stepped back, but it was too late. Rachel rushed down the steps. There was no way out. The kitchen door was bolted on the inside, and the wall that supported the stairs to the front of the house was behind them. But Hero wasn't afraid of Rachel. Rachel stood at the far end of the area, arms folded.

'How's your shoulder, Rachel? I hear you've been crying to your mother how it's my fault. Well, I never so much as laid one finger on you, but I might have to make up for it now!' Hero clenched her fists and breathed in, ready to breathe out and sock Rachel hard.

Rachel stood still, she didn't move an inch, she just sneered. Hero took one step forward, drew her right arm back and . . .

'Stop it!' Daniel had caught her arm. 'Don't!'

Hero shrugged Daniel off and Rachel laughed.

'What did you do that for?' Hero could feel her face growing hot.

'I don't want any more of this fighting.'

'I never started it,' Hero said to Dan.

'Trouble? And I thought you two were such good friends,' Rachel smirked.

'Leave it, Rach!' Dan said. 'I want this sorted properly, no lying, no fighting.'

Hero moved closer to Rachel. She wanted to wipe that smile off her smug face completely.

'Enough!' Dan's voice was so loud the girls both stopped.

The kitchen door behind them was hastily unbolted and Mrs Isaacs took one look at Hero and ran back into the house shouting, 'Mrs Silver! Mrs Silver! That girl is here! That girl! Down in the area!'

'Thank you, Daniel.' Hero stepped back and sighed. 'I am utterly skewered now, wouldn't you say?'

Rachel put both hands on her hips and laughed. 'Hero da Costa! Betrayed by your only friend.'

'I never betrayed anyone!' Daniel was furious.

'Shut up, Rachel!' Hero turned to Dan. 'Daniel, look,' she whispered, 'we can still get away. I could push your sister over and we'd be up the area steps before your mother has wobbled near enough to catch us.'

'Hero, I want to do something right! I want them,' he pointed at Rachel, 'to do something right! Don't you see! This morning Mother and Father swore to me they'd called the auction off. I want to make sure they keep their promises.'

Hero was frantic. 'But I've just told you! The auction's still on!'

'And if I can stop it your troubles are over, yes?'

'Yes, but they'll not listen to you, will they?'

Daniel looked very grim. Hero kept thinking that if they'd started running when she'd said, they would be halfway to St Paul's by now. 'I'll make them, don't you see?'

Hero didn't, and now Mrs Silver had burst through the kitchen door, shouting. 'Right! Mrs Isaacs, fetch me the yard broom!'

Mrs Isaacs scurried away, and Daniel stepped forward. 'Mother, Mother, wait please! Hero's not come to harm any of us.' Mrs Silver's eyes were locked on Hero. 'Just let's come in and settle this straight, please? No chains, no brooms, no shouting, just the truth,' he stared at his mother, 'from everyone.'

Mrs Silver's eyes flickered. 'She can't be trusted, Daniel. She's barely civilized.'

'Mother, you don't believe that! This is the same girl who ate with us every New Year not long ago. Mother, she is part of this family, please?'

Mrs Silver looked at Rachel, and back to Hero.

'I don't think I want to do this, Dan!' Hero whispered.

Mrs Silver spoke. 'It may be said she was born of my cousin, Lily Juliet, but as to whether she is bound by blood to our family . . . I can safely say that she has forfeited any familial rights—'

Daniel rolled his eyes. 'Mother!'

'Look!' She pulled Daniel close, the bruise on her face had faded, but only a little. 'See what she did to me? That girl!' She stabbed with her finger in Hero's direction.

'You slapped me first!'

'For your own good! Everything we ever did was for your own good! But would you listen? No, not a word!'

'But you wanted Pa back in Barbados!'

'What would you rather have, what would any girl rather have? A decent start in life, a job, a little money, a reputable family background, or—' she waved her finger at Dan and Hero both opening their mouths to speak like wet fish '—or growing up in a dissolute and immoral fighters' ken like The Feathers with a Negro for a father!'

Rachel nodded and Daniel ushered everyone inside.

Hero was getting so angry she thought she'd have to hit her again. She felt her fists tensing, but stopped herself. Dan was right, it was exactly what they expected; Hero da Costa, size of a giant, goes around throwing punches. She forced herself to breathe deep breaths, to make the anger go away.

'I was perfectly happy at The Feathers, and my father

is the best father I could have. You didn't do any of this for me, you did it to fill your own pockets!'

Now Mrs Silver was gaping.

Dan smiled. He walked over to Hero and stood next to her.

'I've not finished yet. I know Grandpa wanted us to have The Feathers, you know that too!' Hero pointed for effect and Mrs Silver half sat, half collapsed into a chair. 'I hope his spirit haunts you for the rest of your days!' Hero almost wanted to smile, she was enjoying letting her words do the fighting. 'I bet you don't mind lying to me, I'm just a nigger girl, an embarrassment, but you even lied to your own son!'

Mrs Silver gasped and began fanning herself. Rachel rushed to her side. 'Mother!'

'Shall we go, Dan?'

Daniel stood by the area door, smiling. 'I'm away then, Mother, Rachel. You'll know where to find me!'

'But, Daniel,' wailed Mrs Silver, 'you promised you'd stay!'

'You promised to cancel the auction.'

'But I need your father and a lawyer, it needs to be done properly!'

Daniel hesitated. 'Hero, if we can get her to do it, to really cancel that auction, we're safe, your father's got his inn back and everyone's happy!'

'I don't trust her an inch, Dan. I say we get out of here now and let Pa and Cuffay sort it out.'

Rachel was fanning her mother, leaning close. Hero didn't like the look of them; the sooner she was out of here the better she would feel. She opened the area door. 'Come on, Dan, let's go.'

'Wait, Hero. I'll get her to sign something, I'll do it now, there's some paper upstairs.' And he ran up the stairs at the back of the kitchen.

Mrs Silver was still sitting at the kitchen table. 'Don't go, son! Don't go!'

Mrs Silver sat in the kitchen chair like a toad by the side of a puddle, thinking deep dark thoughts, Hero thought, looking at her. It made Hero feel distinctly uncomfortable.

Rachel rubbed her mother's back. Mrs Isaacs came down from upstairs with the broom but Mrs Silver waved her away. 'So,' Mrs Silver sat up, 'happy now, are you? Ruined my family, your father did, never thought of that, did you? Your mother was a sweet girl, younger than me if she'd lived; marrying your father was the start of the end. Look at us! Look at us!' She clung to Rachel. 'Almost ruined, no warehouse! Uncle Reuben had it in for us and that's the truth.' She hugged Rachel, and Hero swore they were whispering.

Hero could hear Daniel upstairs moving around; she wished he'd hurry up. She moved nearer to the area door, in case she needed a fast exit. He seemed to be up there for ever. Hero could hear him banging around—surely a pen and paper never took that long to find.

Daniel came down, face shining. 'I've got everything!'

'But, Dan, it won't mean anything if it's not witnessed.' Hero had listened to enough legal talk to have learnt something.

Daniel didn't seem to care. 'We'll just get Mother to sign it and then we'll be off.' Hero thought she saw him wink.

'No! It needs to be someone big, someone . . . someone like the rabbi or an alderman. Otherwise it's worth nothing!'

Mrs Silver smiled at her son. Hero could tell from looking at her that she wasn't worried, that this was a waste of time.

Mrs Silver put her hand to her throat and pressed the necklace she wore between her fingers. 'Daniel, my Daniel, we're not out to swindle anyone, we're just looking after our interests.'

There was a noise upstairs, the front door. Men's voices.

'Father!' Daniel looked scared. The pen in his hand fell to the floor. Mrs Silver smiled.

'Let's go, Dan!'

'I think we should!'

Hero hadn't been watching Rachel. Suddenly Rachel was swinging at her with a large metal skillet. 'Hero! Duck!'

Hero ducked. The flying pan swung half an inch above her head. Rachel, holding it two handed, readied herself to swing it the other way. Hero walloped her in the stomach and Rachel folded in half, all breath knocked out of her. She fell down, dropping the cast-iron pan on the floor. It clanged like the heaviest bell in the tower at St Anne's, a low vibrating sound, then smashed on the stone tiles, shards of iron flying everywhere.

'Oh, my God! Benjamin! Benjamin! Come quick.'

Hero grabbed Dan and pulled him up after her out of the kitchen and up the area steps, along White Kennet Street and didn't stop until she reached Ludgate Circus. She was breathing so hard she couldn't speak for a good ten minutes.

Daniel was grinning.

'What's so funny?' Hero panted.

Daniel put his hand inside his jacket. He had a bundle of legal papers, tied in lawyers' pink-red ribbon, in his hand.

'So?'

'From Father's office,' said Daniel. 'There will be no auction now.'

'Do I look like a cake-head to you, Daniel Silver! Are you sure?'

Daniel nodded. Hero looked at the papers. She couldn't read them either; more squiggles, like all the other ones.

'Are you really sure, Dan? I mean, we ought to check with Cuffay first.'

'I've never been so sure in my whole life.'

Hero whooped so loud half Fleet Street turned to look.

Hero took Daniel by the hands and swung him around. 'I could kiss you, Daniel Silver!'

Daniel went the same pink as the lawyers' tape and headed towards Soho as fast as he could.

FOURTEEN

Daniel was right. The papers he'd taken proved the Silvers had acted unlawfully, and proved that Grandpa Reuben's will was sound. Cuffay slapped Daniel so hard on the back that his knees gave way and he ended up on the floor. Hero didn't stop grinning for a week.

Now there was only the matter of re-fitting The Feathers. The Lloyds and some of Pa's neighbours pitched in with wood for tables, paint, and polish; Cuffay came in as partner, and with his money workmen were hired, new windows were put in, and a fine new inn sign painted, edged in gilt, of three curling ostrich feathers. They'd set the date for re-opening on the first Saturday in July and the three weeks before opening were some of the busiest Hero had ever known. Cleaning mostly, polishing the brass rail on the counter and the new doorhandles and the new mirrors bought to hang behind the bar. Sweeping up the mess the workmen had made only to have a new pile twice the size to clear up the next day.

Simon Peter was well enough to help with the building work and Daniel and Ez painted and ran errands and washed down the counter. Hero hadn't felt so happy for a long time.

There were so many in The Feathers on opening night the crowd spilled into the yard and filled Old Compton Street. All the swell mob were there fresh from an all-day bout between Giant Jack Farrer and The Killarney Mule, Harry Donnelly, at Hertford. Giant Jack had won and the young gentlemen had pockets full of winnings which they spent on drink and tipping Ned who was playing the only tunes he knew, 'Lilliburlero' and 'The Girl I left Behind' over and over on the fiddle. Sara counted four lords and an earl in the saloon bar alone.

Every one of the Grandsons of Africa were there too, even William Julius, who was loudest exclaiming John da Costa the finest man in London town. Hero didn't know how Pa could forgive him, but he took her aside quietly, telling her grudges were bad for the soul. Hero had never worked so hard in her life, nor Ez or Daniel who were refilling tankards and jugs again and again and again.

They didn't start shutting up until after midnight. Pa had to help William Julius out and when he couldn't find a link boy, Pa said he'd walk him home. He leant against Pa's arm and declared that he was his best and oldest, even his truest, friend and Hero shook her head as Julius's voice disappeared off into the dark of the night.

It was past one when Hero slid home the shiny new brass bolts on the new dark mahogany doors. She went through to the kitchen with the cash box for Pa to add up the takings when he came home. Then she picked up the broom and some rags and went back to the saloon to help Ez and Dan clear up.

'Honest!' Daniel stopped sweeping up the ale-sodden sawdust from the floor and wiped his brow with his shirtsleeve. 'I'd never have thought that fine gentlemen could make such a great mess!'

'You're lucky, not a one of them pissed in the saloon tonight.' Hero picked up four tankards and returned them to the counter. 'Are you still sure you want to be working here?'

Daniel grinned. He was about to answer when there was an almighty crash and a lump of stone, Daniel later identified it as a cobblestone dug up from the Charing Cross Road, came spinning through the window and smashed into one of the new tables.

'They're throwing rocks at us!'

'Ez, run upstairs, see if you can see anything!'

Ez hadn't come down when a shout came from outside.

'Da Costa!' It was Tyndall, Hero had not forgotten that voice. 'Da Costa, think it's all all right do ya?' The mahogany doors rattled. 'Think you're all right in there?'

'I thought Tyndall was in Barbados by now!' Dan said.

'So did I!'

'How long before your pa's back?'

Hero shook her head. She was thinking. Pa may be half an hour. In that time Tyndall and his mate would have smashed every single window in the place and battered the doors down and made off with the takings. She ran upstairs to where Ez was watching them. It was Tyndall and the other one, Webster. They were drunker than lords; Webster was almost falling over. She ran back to Daniel who was piling chairs up against the door.

'Move them!'

'Are you mad!'

'They're so drunk we can manage them easy, the three of us. Let them in! They won't be expecting it!'

Daniel didn't look as though he believed her. Outside the men were swearing and cursing themselves straight to hell. Ez came down and started helping Dan move the chairs.

'Maybe the nightwatchmen will turn up and send them packing,' Dan said.

'Yes, and in the meantime they've broken every window in the place!' Dan and Ez looked at each other. There was no point in arguing. 'Dan, you take the right,' she pointed at him, 'and Ez, the left.' Hero knew she was scared; these men had practically killed her, would have and worse. If this doesn't work . . . don't think about it, she said to herself, it will work. She breathed deep and picked up two stone bottles full of ale from the counter.

'When I say open, open!'

She held one in each hand, tight around the neck, like the Indian clubs jugglers use. She felt the weight of the bottles in her hands; she knew she'd hit them both hard, she'd been wanting to do this for a very long time.

'Open!' Hero shouted.

The doors flew open and Tyndall, red-faced, flew in. Hero, standing by Dan at the side of the door, walloped him hard over the head, so hard she heard the crack of the bottle against his skull. Tyndall collapsed onto his knees, groaned, and fell sideways across the doorway. Ez cheered from behind the door.

Webster, storming in directly behind him, fell over Tyndall's prone body and Hero brought the second bottle down on the back of his fat red neck. It was over so quickly, Hero still held a bottle in each hand, her heart still racing. Ez gave Webster an extra kick in the side. 'That's for my mate Simon Peter!' But Hero doubted he even felt it.

The two men lay in a heap in the open doorway of The Feathers. Outside London was almost asleep, a fat full moon hanging over the city. Hero stood back, grinning. 'Right, boys!' she said, putting the two bottles down on the nearest table. 'Let's tie 'em up.'

It took a while to drag the men inside so that the doors would shut. Hero took one leg and Dan and Ez the other and they pulled each man in turn across the threshold. Tyndall moaned so Hero hit him again, 'Just in case!'

Ez fetched some rope from the yard and Hero found a belt in Pa's room and belted the two men's legs together. 'They'll not get far like that.'

Dan was bending over Webster tying his hands. 'This one has the smell of a tannery, or our Sam's napkin.' He wrinkled his nose. 'Something or someone's pissed on him and that's for sure!'

Hero looked across and saw Webster was still wearing the same jacket as the night in the rag warehouse. She remembered how scared she'd been of Tyndall and Webster, of the Silvers, and of never seeing Pa ever again. She thought she was going to cry; she felt a choky catch at the back of her throat.

'Hero, are you all right?' Dan asked.

'Never better!' Hero said wiping her face. 'Let's clean this place up.'

When Pa came back, Ez had already gone for the nightwatchman and Daniel was sweeping up the shards of glass from the broken window. 'Hero, are you all right! My God! What in the name of heaven has happened here?' Pa stepped over the bodies in the saloon. Hero was in the kitchen calmly making coffee.

'It's fine, Pa, everything's just as it should be.' She smiled.

It took another hour before the nightwatchmen came and took their report, then Ez and Dan went to bed. Pa stayed up to count the takings and Hero made him a late supper—leek soup and bread—like old times. She yawned.

'You're tired, my love, go to bed,' Pa said.

'Pa, one thing, before I go up.'

'Hmm?' Pa stretched in the hard kitchen chair.

'Tell me, what was it like before you came to London?'

Pa smiled.